I0738757

SURFACE CHILDREN

A Book of Short Stories by Dean Blake

SURFACE CHILDREN
A BOOK OF SHORT STORIES

* * * * *

Dean Blake

Copyright © 2017
Discover more work at generationend.com

ISBN 9780992369019

This is a work of fiction. Names, characters, places and incidents either are the product of the author's imagination or are used fictitiously. Any resemblance to actual persons, living or dead, events or locales is entirely coincidental.

This book is licensed for your personal enjoyment only. No part of this book may be reproduced in any form by any electronic or mechanical means including photocopying, recording or information storage and retrieval without permission in writing from the author. Thank you for respecting the hard work of this author.

If you enjoyed this book, please don't forget to review it on Goodreads.

* * * * *

For the mirrors above our bathroom sinks.

SURFACE CHILDREN

A BOOK OF SHORT STORIES

Table Of Contents

Eva, Part One:
Always Eighteen

What made Eva special to begin with was that she looked good. She had long legs, for one, and she liked to wear teasingly short skirts, which was even better. I guess that's why I immediately told her everything good about myself.

"I'm going to be a famous novelist!" I yelled at her when we first met. "A fucking wealthy novelist!"

For some stupid reason it worked, because she came over the night after wearing a bunny costume that came complete with bunny ears and a fluffy white short skirt with a fluffy rabbit tail – it was Easter, and she wanted to dress for the occasion.

"Let's go to your bathroom," she said when everything became dark.

I was eighteen when I met her and she was sixteen turning seventeen. I don't remember her being that particularly funny and I don't think that, from the moral side of things, she was that good of a person. But her legs were perfect, and she looked like one of those girls someone like me realistically shouldn't have been able to be with. But I did end up with her and for a while, it was great. Even up to now, I wonder why the hell she picked me. Maybe she liked me because she was young and still partially innocent, or maybe she liked me because I was simply there. It certainly couldn't have had anything to do with my looks or personality.

The problem was, I never got a book deal and I never became wealthy. I didn't succeed in anything, for that matter. Sooner or later we started fighting. Sooner or later she stopped wanting to see me. Sooner or later she stopped calling me back. Sooner or later the cheating began and sooner or later, she was gone.

When you really think about it, Eva was simply a girl I bumped into. If you broke her down to her jewellery and her anatomy and the things she said and the jokes she laughed at and the men she'd kissed and the girls she'd kissed and her parents and her dog and the types of boys who liked to call her phone at night and all that kind of shit, Eva would just be one of many, just as I was one of many. But I still took photographs of her with a smile on my face.

Anyway I hated her, and even if I hated her I started a blog called Always Eighteen about her, and even after years of us not talking, I continued with the blog. Eventually, that blog became Generation End. This book is for those who know my work and for those who are about to get to know my work. It contains stories about Eva and my friends, and it also contains a few stories I've written over the years.

That's about it, really.

The Committee

We started the committee because it was a committee that had to be started, needed to be started.

There was me, there was Robby and there was Kath. We planned for there to be more of us in the future but in the meantime we were happy with just the three of us, and because there were just the three of us we knew that the task we were facing was enormous and bordering on the impossible: our task was to make ourselves, as well as future committee members, look perfect from every angle. No matter what the weather conditions were like.

I was born with a perfect right side profile. Robby looked perfect from the front. Kath looked perfect from behind, from the top left (if she smiled in a certain coy way) and from her direct left. We all looked perfect from the distance... if you didn't squint. But that was it. That was all we had. It was tragic.

"I'm sick of going through hundreds of ugly photos of myself and only finding one or two good ones that happen to be of my right side profile," I told Kath and Robby. "I've even had to change my privacy settings on Facebook so that my friends won't see my disgusting face whenever I'm tagged. We have to do something about this."

"I agree," they both said, nodding in unison. "This is something definitely worth fighting for."

"I'm glad we're all on the same wavelength. And it's not like your thighs are perfect, Kath."

"You know what else?" Kath looked worried.

"What?"

"Your right side profile, Robby's front profile, my top left profile – they're only perfect profiles if we have certain expressions on our faces. How about if we're laughing? How about if we're frowning? How about if we're eating? How about if we're jumping? How about if –"

"You're absolutely right, Kath!" I was genuinely impressed at her insight because she was usually quite stupid. "We have to perfect ourselves on every angle, on every emotion, on every action and on every combination of the three, like if we're smiling and jumping and being seen from the left and right, or smirking and jogging and being observed from below or from above or from the centre left. We have to look good no matter what, on any instance." I suddenly came up with another goal: "I also want to look good to every kind of person in this world. I want rich people to worship our looks just as much as poor people do. I want every straight person and every homo and every white person and every black person and every whatever-the-hell-else is out there to think we look perfect."

"So you even want to get the respect of," Kath lowered her voice, "of Middle Easterners?"

"Of course!" I exclaimed. "We need to be loved by everyone in this world!"

"Wow," Kath was impressed. "Wow."

"There's something else we need to do," I said. "Something very important to society."

"What is it?" They both asked, their breaths held tight.

"We also have to look perfect on our passport photos."

There was a huge gust of silence after this. Kath looked like she was about to cry from the sheer magnitude of the task ahead of us.

Robby realised something. "How do we do it? This sounds really hard and expensive."

We all went quiet for a moment.

"Should we make a deal with the devil?" he suggested. He didn't look too good from where he was sitting.

"Nah," I said. "Remember Mitch? He made a deal with the devil and look at him now."

"He's a total loser," Kath agreed. "I mean, did you see his shoes?"

"He's disgusting."

"Oh!" Kath raised her hand before realising how embarrassing it was to raise your hand in such situations, especially when we could see the stubble on her armpit. She quickly put her hand down. "There's like, a guy. I like, heard about him on the news. He's like, this billionaire who performs these amazing miracles. All you have to do is make a wish and he'll put his hands on you and your wish will come true. We can tell him all about our desires. But I heard he's expensive."

"I don't believe in quick fixes," I declared. "This is going to come out of our own hard work."

And it was hard work. The work was so hard it

almost made me cry. But crying is ugly in most circumstances so I didn't. We worked out several times a day. We stuck by the strictest diets. We hired personal trainers and nutritionists and consumed wheatgrass and apple cider vinegar and barley leaves and spinach and everything that tasted boring or disgusting. We went to posture classes to improve our posture. We went to drama classes to improve our ability to appear confident even if we didn't feel confident. We invested in every fashion magazine and event we could find. We constantly gave each other the most brutally honest constructive criticism anyone could ever imagine. We posted our photos online and asked the world to judge us based on all of our angles and took serious notes on everything they said. We watched popular movies and TV shows from all over the world and took notes on when actors looked their best and most charming. We took videos of ourselves, ensuring that the video camera would focus on us on every single angle and on every single emotion and on every single action stance for as long as possible; we then discussed these angles at length, talking about all the ways we could improve how we looked.

Initially, it felt like playing with a Rubik's Cube for the first time: whenever we'd do something to get one angle of ourselves looking good, such as when styling our hair in such a way to maximise the impact of our front-up-left profile, we discovered that doing so subsequently caused another angle of ourselves, such as the front-centre-right profile, to become drastically uglier than it was if we hadn't styled our hair to improve our front-up-left profile. It was irritating, but we overcame it with a lot of mirror work and exercise and plastic surgery.

Kath smiled at me one morning.

"What the hell do you want?"

She kept smiling. "You look really... good. The differences from the ugly you, and the you now... they're outstanding. I mean, I'm looking at you from what used to be your worst angle, too."

I was about to tell her to shut the hell up until I realised what she said. I gazed into my hand mirror for a few minutes, grinned to look at my teeth from first to last and lowered my head to inspect the top of my hair before carefully putting my mirror away to finally look her over. Surprisingly, I was also impressed at what I was looking at. "You're not so bad yourself. I mean there's a small hair on your eyebrow that needs plucking but other than that..."

"I'm glad you accept me."

"You know you have all these fat ugly guys who always go for girls like you, but then when they get rejected by girls like you they complain that you're a shallow bitch. But why don't they go for ugly girls? Why would a hot girl like a guy who doesn't put as much effort into looking good and looking healthy as much as the girl does? Our personalities are reflected by our looks, and I'm the only person in the world who understands this."

We drove to her shabby little apartment and had some water and did a bit of small talk before going into her smelly little bedroom.

"My brothers used to tease me for having crooked teeth," I said after glancing at the cheap full body mirror leaning against her wall.

She carefully unzipped her dress before also glancing

at the mirror. "Girls used to bully me for my funny chin."

"This girl in primary school dumped me for someone who was taller." I removed my tie.

"A guy dumped me because I refused to wear skirts. 'Why should I choose you when there's someone better looking out there who'd love to wear a skirt?' he asked me. 'It's so much easier to finger a girl with a skirt, and it's hotter. Don't you get how hot it is? Why are you so selfish?'" She removed her earrings, her bracelet, her dress.

"My mother still pinches my cheeks and calls me chubby. It hurts me so much when she does this." I removed my shirt, removed my belt, removed my pants.

"We all used to laugh at this kid with a button nose. We pointed at him and called him piggy. You wouldn't believe how ugly his nose was." She unclasped her bra. "He looked like Voldemort, but worse."

"There was this girl we teased for having patchy skin and funny lips. We kept telling her she looked like a monkey because it was true." I removed my boxer shorts.

"I can't sleep until I know I've done at least a hundred sit ups." She slowly pulled her panties down.

"I can't go out unless what I'm wearing guarantees that everyone who sees me will instantly be attracted to me."

"I'm going to commit suicide if I gain more wrinkles than I do now." She knelt down.

I touched her face and kissed her forehead. "I hope you do, because wrinkles are a terrible disease. Run your fingers down my toned, but not *too* toned six pack, like in the movies."

"I really want to video my top-up-right angle right

now and see how it looks when I move my head."

She was the first person I'd ever slept with, and things were pretty good for a while until three months later, when I started to feel more secure about myself around her. That was when I started working out a little less, when I started looking at myself a little less, when I started swearing at her and Robby a little less. All I wanted to do was call her and ask her how she was and yell at her if I found out that she was speaking to another guy. I was even pathetic enough to say that I wanted children. In the end, she broke up with me and then hooked up with Robby, who was by then the most good looking guy on the planet and in the history of the planet. He even had his own Wikipedia page. I wouldn't stop throwing mirrors at him, so both he and Kath kicked me out of the committee.

I went home in shame. I looked at my perfectly clean mobile phone to search for friends to call for comfort and realised that I no longer had any, because the ones I used to be friends with never believed in using the right moisturiser. I wanted to cry, but of course I didn't. *Why was this happening to me?* I thought to myself. The world hated me, even though I'd done nothing wrong.

After a few weeks of horrible depression I had an epiphany: what was the media teaching me? I'd forgotten to listen to the media, because, as I used to repeatedly tell Kath and Robby, "The media provides the only source of honesty in this world because we're the ones who created it in the first place." After buying as many celebrity gossip magazines and fashion magazines as I could afford, I found myself inspired again: I was going to change the world by making myself perfect in every way. Even more perfect than Robby.

I put in an extraordinary amount of hard work into perfecting my appearance, even more hard work than I did when I was with Kath and Robby. Thankfully, it wasn't too long before I noticed the changes. Soon, the mere act of me being seen by someone caused them to burst out into a round of applause. They did this at any angle they saw me at and at any expression I had on my face and at any action I was performing; I'd improved myself so much that even if you saw me from behind, you'd instantly assume that I was the most perfect looking person in the world. But that wasn't enough. I wanted people to burst out in tears of joy whenever they saw me, not just make shitty little claps. So I worked harder and harder until one day it finally came true: people would burst out in tears of joy whenever they saw me. From my perfection I became deliriously famous, and from my fame I became deliriously wealthy, and from my wealth I married a deliriously beautiful woman who was loyal and tender and patient and shut up when it was appropriate for her to shut up; she helped me become a better man and she helped me have two kids: one very handsome boy (older) and one very good looking girl (younger). We also adopted an adopted Vietnamese son of two very famous models who became heroin addicts and died in a tragic car accident. Whatever he lacked in looks we made up with expensive, trendy clothing and expensive, trendy hairstyles. Plus plastic surgery.

The money kept pouring in, and with that money we were able to be photographed with famous people (such as the president of the United States), we modeled for

Givenchy and Gucci and Comme des Garçons, we were able to put the kids through school (even the adopted one, believe it or not); we joined country clubs, bought properties all over the world, and most importantly, donated considerably to charity: we restored villages, we found the cure for herpes, we helped a bunch of African kids gain weight, and last but not least, we bought the committee over and made sure Robby and Kath would never be noticed by anyone again and in fact would die of something embarrassing, like yeast infections or homelessness or something. And it was great because they did end up dying of something embarrassing like yeast infections or homelessness or something.

Life became photos and videos and flashes and positive, worthwhile gossip. It was a rush. A truly enjoyable rush. Thanks to inspiring hard work, unbeatable patience and my perfect looks, my family and I and the entire world have since lived happily ever after.

Los Angeles Angie

Note: I suppose I ended up writing the letter to him because I had nothing much else to do, and I know for sure that he can't delete letters like he deletes his emails: he has to open them and then he has to scan over them and then he has to place them down and then he has to continue his day.

Anyway in the letter I tried my best not to write about Angie at all, but by the end of the letter, by the end of all my surface blabber, I couldn't help but slip her name in there.

"So anyway, how's Angie? Is she still a bitch?" I wrote before quickly writing about something else. I felt dirty.

When I first met Angie one of my sunglass lenses popped out. I walked up to her after class and started talking to her because she was pretty. As I spoke to her, one the lenses popped out and onto the ground, shattering everywhere. She laughed and told me that I was embarrassing.

Eventually, we left the campus and walked along the street and she asked me, "What are we doing?"

"We're walking along the damn street. Now what's your number?"

She gave me her number and when I called her at

night she told me about this guy she was in love with. She even blogged about how she was in love with him. In her blog, she wrote, "I'm in love with him."

I told her that falling in love is interesting, I suppose, but there are other, far more interesting things out there.

"Like what? What's far more interesting than falling in love?" She seemed genuinely curious.

"How the hell should I know?"

She then told me that she'd changed. I told her that I wouldn't know if she'd changed or not because I'd just met her. But she insisted that she'd changed. She told me that she used to be fat and dorky but now she was skinny and spent most of her time going out with friends. She told me that she never used to swear but now all she does is swear. She told me that she smokes now, too. She told me to call her Los Angeles Angie.

The next day she showed me her mobile phone with the photos of the guy she was in love with. He had stylish hair. She told me that he was Japanese but we both knew that he wasn't Japanese. She told me that they were both planning to go to Japan to teach primary school children.

"I won't be allowed into clubs there because you have to be twenty one, and I'm only eighteen," she said.

"If you're eighteen and I'm twenty-two and we're classmates, then that must mean I'm…"

She laughed at that. We walked to this bar that had happy hour going on and she asked me, "Does this bar have happy hour going on?"

And I said, "Yeah. It has happy hour going on."

And we drank during this happy hour. We drank quite a lot, and for the first time in my life it actually was a happy hour. She pulled her legs up so she could sit cross-legged on the bar's leather couch and pulled a cigarette out of her small expensive-looking black purse and lit it and inhaled and exhaled and tapped. There was no ashtray because it's illegal to smoke in bars now, and after realising this she killed the cigarette into her empty glass of ice cubes.

She was drunk – while I was in the toilet she stumbled over to a group of big guys who were confident at playing pool. I spotted her right after one of them leant over and kissed her; she kissed him back.

I pointed at her before dragging her out of there.

"You cheater! I can't believe you just cheated."

She just smiled. We walked to the car park. She was a rich kid so she had her own car park in the city. She pulled out her clinking bundle of keys and other things and pressed a button and her BMW beeped in response. We stepped inside: the car had leather seats and a big television screen. I couldn't believe it. It was like I was with a celebrity.

"I'll, I'll drive you home," she slurred. Her head was bobbing slightly.

"Fine!" My head was also bobbing slightly.

On the drive home she asked me what would happen if there was a sudden crash, if because she was drunk she wanted to speed more, and she did speed more, and she kept speeding and speeding and eventually swerving and swerving and the glorious BMW became so wild and so liberated and so sure of itself that it wanted to crash into something as equally beautiful and as equally confident just to see what would happen, and so it did: it smashed against a giant statue of a horse and a soldier sitting gallantly on that horse; there was an earthquake of a noise, time lost its appeal, there was dinting and there was shuddering and there was screaming and anyone who would've seen the event would've been momentarily silent, pondering but not pondering at all: the catastrophe would've been immense, it would've been pretty interesting, it would've been one of those things you'll use as a conversation starter in parties for years to come if you made it out of it alive.

But the accident never happened and she drove me home safely. I wanted to put my hand on her leg and feel her up and kiss her, but I did nothing. We barely said goodbye. After that, for twelve months, at least, she actually did remain in love with him; they never went to Japan but they did have sex a lot of times and she kept blogging about him and posting up photos of him and the two of them together. Los Angeles Angie and I drifted apart and instead, for a while, anyway, her love became my best friend and I became his. Eventually I stopped thinking about her or trying to text her; I learnt things about the world and I grew up and matured and de-matured and fell in love a couple of times and fell on my face a couple of times. I tried new things and stayed with some old things and sometimes I'd look at photos from the past, and when I would I'd get sentimental and write more letters such as the one I'd written just then.

Eva, Part Two:
Where It Was Said

Eva first told me that she loved me while we were in my bedroom. We were sweating, and her hair was still the way it was and we were two months into whatever we were doing and she whispered, "I love you."

"What?"

"I don't expect you to say it back or anything like that, but I want to get it out there. I want the universe to hear it."

I sort of mumbled something back, and she held my face and smiled and kissed my forehead. She let go and thought about something: she tilted her head downwards and bit her bottom lip and I lightly pulled her chin up so that she could look at me front on and she held both of my hands and her eyes were perfect; a bit of light from somewhere outside gave her face a shy texture.

Something inside me changed in that instant, but I didn't tell her that. Instead I said nothing, and after about an hour or so we went outside to rent a DVD or something like that and afterwards she asked me to take a photo of her posing in front of my house. I smiled and told her to stand still.

The Worst Thing Jude
Has Ever Done

I think what makes me special from most guys is that I've never really masturbated before. It's true. The link isn't there. Don't ask me why, but I just don't have that need to stare at a computer and tug myself.

Dean and all of that met me on Wednesday night, at Eagle Street, under the precursor that I had some terrible news to tell them. But I changed my mind at the last minute and told them something completely bogus and decided, instead, to focus on this other girl I invited who came to meet us a bit later, Megan. I met her at my uncle's party last Saturday night and we'd been texting each other repeatedly since.

While in bed she told me that it was fine that I didn't bring protection, that I could just go on her stomach. So I did. After I watched her giggle and wipe I walked to her balcony and smiled and listened to the quiet hums of everything outside.

...

On Thursday I drove to the Gold Coast with a few friends and walked along the beach, kicking a ball around and talking about nothing in particular. I felt bored, so I told my friends that I'd shout them to the shooting range. It ended up costing me over two thousand dollars but it was worth it: we spent over an hour shooting rifles, magnums, shotguns, revolvers. Afterwards, I called the doctor's place and didn't say anything – I just listened to the receptionist repeatedly asking, *Hello?* until she hung up. One day, I'd love to use a grenade launcher to blow up an entire building.

In the evening I met Megan again. She was wearing expensive-looking lingerie that I bet an ex-boyfriend bought for her. I wrapped my hands around the back of her head and made her kneel.

...

I felt incredibly bored on Friday morning and spent about three hours looking for decent flights to Hawaii online. I then looked at photos of Hawaii and decided that I wouldn't feel any different there. I then spent about an hour looking for decent flights to Europe but then changed my mind again. I then looked at new cars, but I just convinced my dad to buy another C-Class last year. This thought suddenly came to me: there are so many women out there, so many women I'll never get to have sex with.

I drove to Olja's house and she let me in and, just like the other day, ended up crying and constantly telling me that she was sorry. I stood up and put my hand on her shoulder and told her that the results haven't arrived yet, that you never know, that miracles happen to good people like me and her. *But his results have arrived,* she insisted, *and goodness knows how many times we'd been with each other, how many times I've been with you without protection. Don't you understand how awful HIV is, Jude? Don't you understand how both our lives are ruined? You don't get anything, do you? I'm so sorry, oh fuck I'm so sorry. I should've had myself tested before I met you I'm so sorry.* I walked to the kitchen and made us both a glass of water and when it was quiet I leant towards her and we made out but I stopped once she started crying again, and I asked her why she wouldn't let me finger her as we were both going to die anyway.

I drove for about forty-five minutes to the Biala City Community Health Centre. I took an elevator to the free sexual health clinic, took a few pamphlets, read them, put them back. I looked at the types of people waiting there: someone in a business suit, a young couple who looked poor, some guy in a black shirt with large earphones on. I drove off to my friend's place and we spent the rest of the evening drinking and smoking and watching horror movies with some of their new neighbours.

...

I walked into my dad's office on Saturday morning and lay on his leather couch as he typed on his computer. He smiled and asked me how I was and I said I was good and he resumed typing. I picked up a magazine and flicked through it, pretending to read through the articles. Once in a while one of his employees would come in and they'd talk about something boring or complain about someone from another department. Or once in a while my dad would answer his mobile, stand up, and walk out of the room and then come back in about ten minutes later and ask me if I wanted a drink. I smelt my shirt: it smelt like the cigarettes from last night. *I'll text you if I'm coming home tonight,* I told him as I stood up and walked out.

...

I met Dean in the evening and like always he looked tired and was incredibly negative about the world. I told him that I slept with Megan and he shrugged and asked me what was new, so I also shrugged and ordered us both drinks.

We were both drunk by eight o'clock. I considered telling him the news about Olja, but changed my mind because it was pointless anyway. Dean walked off towards somewhere and I sat around for a while, just listening to all the noises in the background. I wondered what it'd be like if I was sick in hospital, if Dean would visit me right away. I pulled my phone out of my pocket and texted Megan that I was sleeping in at home tonight. I then called Ariel, this girl who's supposedly not a prostitute or an escort but wouldn't mind having sex with me for a few hundred dollars anyway. *Wear that cute little skirt you wore last month,* I told her and hung up.

I took Ariel back to a friend's place. She looked sort of cheap, but she was pretty in her own way. We joked around for a while, and I even managed to convince her that you can buy a cure for Cancer in Thailand. She went down on me twice, swallowing both times, and I paid her about four hundred dollars and we spent the rest of the evening watching the Sopranos on my friend's computer and talking about a variety of things: the new Britney video, her friend who backstabbed her, getting IPL treatment, guys with plucked eyebrows. I told her that I was afraid of certain things and that I had a few ambitions in life but I was also completely bored. I asked her what she'd say if I gave her a disease that made her sick, like really, really sick. She smiled and said that she'll never let a man make her sick. When she fell asleep I ran my fingers along her hair and listened to her breathing softly.

In the morning I drove to Megan's house and she made me breakfast. Smiling, she told me that she liked me. I smiled and told her that I liked her too. I picked her up from the floor and we repeatedly made love until the evening. *It's okay*, she whispered, *I'll just take a morning after pill tomorrow.*

...

Sundays are a hit and miss for me. Sometimes I'm completely relaxed and completely hopeful. Sometimes I'm tense. I spent most of the morning on my bed, bored, looking up at my phone while scrolling up and down my Facebook newsfeed.

...

I visited Olja on Monday because she said she had bad news.

I opened the door and was greeted with a slap on the face followed by another slap. She called me a fucker and repeatedly swore at me. She grabbed me by my hair and threw me inside. Breathing hard, she pointed at me and called me an evil bastard cunt. I'd never been called an evil bastard cunt before, so I broke out in laughter. *Evil bastard cunt?* I pointed back at her and laughed. *So you heard? So he told you?* I kept asking her and she said *yes* and kicked me in the ribs. I stood up and, after a while of wincing and breathing hard against her table, I tried to kiss her but she pushed me away and told me to fuck off. *It's not funny. You think HIV is funny? I can't believe you were both in on this. You know I spoke to my parents about it? You know I had to get a fucking blood test? You know how much I cried and what I put my loved ones through?* She was about to slap me again but I raised my fist at her and she flinched. I laughed and said, *You know it's your fault for not waiting for your blood test results, right?*

I called her ex-boyfriend on the drive home and we both laughed about how she reacted. *I can't believe she genuinely thought you had AIDS*, I said. We spoke some more until he asked me for some money, *for, you know, the prank*. I told him, *Sure,* without asking for his bank details and hung up.

    ...

On Tuesday I met Megan by that café in New Farm. She was wearing something she borrowed from her sister, which I told her actually looked better on her sister. She laughed and told me that I was silly, thinking that I was actually joking.

Megan thinks that she's a good person. Megan thinks

that I'm a good person. We both think that we're good people. Our parents probably sometimes think we're good people, too. I wondered what it would be like to have sex with a half African half Mexican girl. I told Megan that I wanted to have sex with her in a bathroom somewhere and she scowled and asked me, *Are you kidding me?* And I got mad, threw some cash at her, gave her the finger and drove off, leaving her there with her overpriced meal.

I called her twenty times in the evening until she finally picked up. I told her that I was sorry for reacting the way I did, and that I had just found out that I had AIDS, and she kept asking me if I'm kidding and, grinning, I told her that I wasn't and she broke down crying.

...

I wonder how life will end. I don't mean my life, but everyone else's. I wonder if everything will suddenly come to an unexpected halt, or if everything will die gradually. I don't really care either way. When everything disappears, where will I go? What will I do? I don't remember what I think about when I first wake up in the morning, and I don't remember what I think about right before I sleep. But it doesn't matter, because what I think about isn't even that important.

One Hundred Sixty Kilograms

I was born into the world not knowing that I'd never meet my father. My mother passed away when I was fifteen, two years after kicking me out of home. I have two younger sisters and a few other half-siblings that I've never met. Most of the time I work ninety hours a week and don't feel tired, mainly because of my diet and also because life is a job and you'll only ever get promoted in the world if you work hard and work smart and stay positive and ask the universe for success again and again and again.

I'm twenty-two years old. I rarely went to school. I make an average of nine hundred and ninety thousand dollars a year mainly through my online sports business and my bottom line is only increasing. I have five employees, all Indian and all living overseas – I've never even seen them, and that's perfect. My mentor, who I pay around twenty thousand dollars a month to receive advice from, recommended that I shift from working ninety hours a week on my business to hiring someone who would manage it instead – this would allow me to concentrate on other projects and acquisitions, creating even more money for my wallet. She said that I should then invest in real estate with my extra income to generate a portfolio and enhance my wealth further, because, after all, your wealth is measured by your holdings. I told my mentor to go fuck herself.

Every day, except Saturday, I eat or drink this: thirty egg whites, oats, protein bars, broccoli, cauliflower, wheatgrass, barley grass, spirulina, chicken breast steaks, fish steaks, almonds, fish oil. This diet minimises the fat in my body and keeps me lean, strong, toned, alert, energetic. I don't care if it makes me fart a lot, all that I care about is that it makes me athletic. Some people hate sport but I think sport is a wonderful thing. It demonstrates self-discipline. It demonstrates ambition. It demonstrates drive. If you could see the intense training regimes of the world's greatest athletes, you'd think that people are aliens, aliens with large heads, large eyes, superpowers – and then you'd want to be an alien just like them because they can do anything and have sex with whoever the hell they want because they're filthy rich, and it's ideal to be filthy rich. Sometimes I vomit while working out. Sometimes the pain in my back is so intense that I think it'll explode. I've had both my knees reconstructed. I have to see a physio at least once a week. I nearly lost a foot during a bike accident in a triathlon. My favourite workout is the bench press: it's original, it's classic, it's simple. I want to bench one hundred sixty kilograms while maintaining my weight of seventy-five kilograms. Every morning, when I look at the mirror, I see imperfection, and this turns me on because I believe imperfection is brilliant: it gives me a goal to obtain, it motivates me to become healthier and more toned every day. Sometimes I love life so much I feel dizzy.

Sometimes I love life so much I vomit all over the bathroom floor.

It was eight in the evening and I'd just finished installing a gym into one of my uncle's rooms. I liked my uncle because he took care of my siblings and I when my parents didn't. He's ten years older than I am and also successful, even if successful in all the wrong ways.

"Want a drink?"

"You only have alcohol," I said. "I'm telling you, man, if you don't want to work out with me, let me hook you up with a good PT. He'll motivate you to get in shape and stop drinking that shit."

"Sex is all you need to get into shape," my uncle laughed and kept drinking. I looked at his small gut as he leant over, splitting some coke on his coffee table, and scowled. "Fuckin' have some, man. And don't say no this time."

"It's time for me to go."

"Just stay, man," my uncle insisted.

"You promised you'd stop offering me drugs."

"Stay for a bit and enjoy your bloody life a bit more." He indicated for me to sit on the couch opposite of him. "I'm lonely tonight and we all barely see you anymore. I miss you, man. I'm sorry I offered you drugs again. Come on, sit, I promise I won't share any of this expensive and highly valuable coke with you again."

I sat down and looked around. "Where are your cousins and that?"

"They're at some Vietnamese chick's party or some shit I don't know." He pointed at the cocaine on the table. "Why don't you just have some?"

"Far out. You just promised that you won't offer me any."

"Fine, you fuckin' health freak." He leant over, snorted and sat back up. "Anyway, I want to tell you why I'm lonely. Besides the fact that we barely see you anymore."

I smiled. "Kitty?"

"Of course, Kitty."

"What about her?"

"I think she's going to break up with me."

I glanced around the large room, at the large chandelier, at the large TV, at the large couches, at the large everything. "That shouldn't be an issue for you. You can get any girl you want."

"But none of them will be like Kitty."

"She's not worth your time," I said. "You're just being a little bitch because you can't accept rejection. Look, there are plenty of girls out there who are better than Kitty. Better tits, better everything. And they'd love to grab a piece of you. Listen, why don't I lend you some of my Anthony Robbins audio CDs? He'll help you stay positive."

My uncle pulled out his mobile, looked at it, texted someone back, then put it back into his pocket. "Maybe you're right, maybe not."

"What's wrong? You guys fight again?"

"Nah, we didn't fight." When I didn't reply, he sighed and looked at the ceiling. "I don't know, man."

"Just tell me what's wrong," I said. "If you didn't fight, then what's wrong?"

"Nothing's wrong," he mumbled.

"You're going to tell me anyway, so just say it now instead of dancing around."

"Fine. I guess you're old enough," he said before pausing for a moment, hesitating, and then eventually deciding to say it: "she doesn't give me blowjobs anymore."

"That's so sad," I laughed. "Boo fucking hoo. You must be so miserable in your large, blowjobless home."

He also laughed, but only partially. "You don't understand, she used to love giving blowjobs. And it's everything else, too. It's like she's drifting. She responds to me with a lot of one liners and isn't as keen on going out with me or coming over as much as she used to. You don't get it. She's the only girl I've never cheated on." My uncle picked up his bottle of beer, took a sip and played with it in his hand. "She's the only girl I've never cheated on," he repeated, making sure that I completely understood the rubbish he was saying. "You wouldn't happen to know anything about her attitude lately do you? Has anyone told you anything?"

I'd never seen that desperate, heartbroken side of my uncle before. He was usually a cocky kind of guy. "Have you asked her what the problem is?"

"Of course I have," he said, putting his bottle of beer back down on the table.

"And what the hell did she say?"

He shrugged as if admitting defeat. "She just keeps telling me nothing's wrong and that she's just been doing a lot of thinking. About what, I don't really know."

"Girls just get like that sometimes. They always think about pointless bullshit."

"How would you know? When's the last time you had a girlfriend?"

I thought about it. "Not too long ago."

"Bullshit," he snickered. "You had your last girl a few years ago."

"Yeah, so what? I don't need a girlfriend."

"Whatever. That's exactly what desperate people say. Sometimes I think you're a fag. In fact I tell everyone you're a fag."

"I seriously don't have enough time for a woman in my life," I said. "I'm too busy making money."

"I work less than you and I make more money than you."

"But unlike you," I said, "I'm less likely to get arrested."

"Fuck you." My uncle picked a pillow up from his couch and threw it straight at me. "I'm serious. I know you want to get rich and believe me, you're already far more richer than I was at your age. But you have to realise what's important, you know? Family, friends, living, breathing, you know? It's not about the money all the time."

"What are you on about? Of course it's about money all the time. Money creates happiness. You want more money. I want more money. Everyone wants more money." We talked for a while longer, my uncle drinking beer and me drinking nothing. We talked about how when I was a kid, I'd cry so hard that he'd sometimes have to beat the shit out of me. We talked about basketball games, drives to the coast, my eighteenth birthday. My sisters and I spent a lot of time with him and his cousins when we were young – he was pretty much like our cool young uncle, or our cool young father, or our cool older brother or however hell else you want to call it. The bottom line is that he was cool and we owed a lot to him.

Sure, we heard rumours about how violent he could actually be towards others. There was one particular rumour his cousins would always tell us about an old friend of his who backstabbed him over some business deal. To seek vengeance, my uncle burnt his house down and then burnt down every home of every person that guy loved – all before running him over and paralysing him for good. My uncle never admitted to or denied these rumours, and this made him even cooler in our eyes. In a way, it made my sisters and I feel as though at least one person in the world – especially someone "cool" like him – actually bothered to protect abandoned kids like us.

"It's late and you're boring me," I finally said. "I have to get up at three in the morning to work tomorrow."

I drove off, thinking about my uncle all the way until I reached Kitty's place. I buzzed in, took the elevator to the third floor and walked to her apartment door. I knocked and she opened it. We looked at each other for a while, just smiling a little and listening to each other breathe.

"Well, here's that thing I was telling you about." I handed her one of my favourite books of all time: *Think and Grow Rich*. "It'll change your life for good."

"Really? Thank you."

"No problems, but make sure to read it twice," I said, remembering what my uncle told me about him not receiving blowjobs anymore. "Anyway, early start tomorrow. I have to rush home."

"Don't be silly, you drove all the way here. Want to grab some coffee?"

"What?" I checked my watch. "Now?"

"It's only ten."

I crossed my head. "I have an early start tomorrow."

"You have an early start every day."

"It's always good to have an early start," I said. "It keeps you energetic –"

"Yeah, yeah, yeah, just come out. Don't be lazy."

"Lazy? I wake up at three to work every day. I'm not fucking lazy."

She giggled. "Yes, you're too lazy to form friendships. You can't get away with living life without actually living it."

"Alright," I said, figuring that I'd make it up by working longer hours the next day. "Let's have a quick coffee."

"Give me a minute." She rushed inside then came back out with some keys and a wallet. She smiled, closed the door, locked it. We headed for the elevator.

"How's your evening?"

"Good," I said.

"Mine too."

"What did you get up to?"

"Just reading a book a friend leant me," she said, "and cleaning, humming to myself, all the simple stuff."

"I like the simple stuff," I said. "Well, as long as that simple stuff helps you make a bit of money in the end."

We drove to a café nearby and as we had coffee she told me about the dog she had when she was growing up. It was a tiny dog at first, but then it grew and grew until it looked dangerous. It was a total prick and she loved that it was a total prick. It chased people and bit people and made them realise that they actually hated dogs. I couldn't care much about dogs and her story bored me, but I smiled as I watched her excitedly describe it. She even showed me a photo of the dog that she kept in her wallet, where the photo had a young version of her grinning at the camera while rubbing the monster's gigantic neck. We also spoke about other things, like parents and shoes and the way people scratch their noses, as well as this time when she went overseas for the first time ever: the way her sister vomited into a bag and the way the air stewardess gave her nice little toys.

Her hair was wavy that evening and it leant towards one side of her face. She had red nails and no eyeliner and her teeth looked perfect, except for one. She was wearing short shorts that night and her legs looked smooth, long, tanned. She was older than I was and it was obvious that she was older than I was through the type of things she liked to speak about and the little lines on her forehead that she couldn't hide with all of her makeup. As Kitty went on and on without shutting up I began thinking about Anita Roddick, founder of the Body Shop. She's a brilliant woman because she puts the idea of human rights into her marketing – because of this she's able to make a lot of good money from people who don't feel guilty (in fact, they feel pretty good) about purchasing her products. I wondered if Kitty could ever possibly become someone as amazing as Anita Roddick. Probably not.

I checked the time and told Kitty that I had to work at three in the morning so I paid the bill and drove her back home. I stayed in my car as she stepped out of it: I looked out of the passenger-side window and she looked back at me, saying nothing; we smiled at each other; she waved and waited for me to leave before heading into her apartment.

I drove home, thinking about nothing in particular, except about this speech I watched online once of the legendary motivational speaker Les Brown, about how you should only hang around people who will elevate you into success. When I parked, I sat in my car, leaning back on my seat and holding the wheel for I don't know how long. I didn't remember ever being awake at that time before. To punish myself for staying up late for all the wrong reasons, I removed my shirt and dug my car key into my bicep. I pressed it as hard as possible and pulled it towards my armpit so that there would be a large and noticeable gash. I screamed in pain while calling myself a lazy, useless, stupid, ungrateful, etc.

The first thing I did when I decided to become successful was to imitate others who were already successful; not just ordinarily successful, either, but immensely successful. I heard that Donald Trump woke up early so from then on I decided to wake up at three every morning. Waking up that early wasn't exactly the easiest thing to do, but eventually, after I got used to all of the fucking pain, I did. Every single day, for the past four years, I had this morning routine: 1. Wake up at three 2. Open my window 3. Meditate 4. Spend ten to forty minutes writing my goals in life while reciting them out loud for the universe to hear them 5. Spend ten minutes in front of the mirror, nude, objectively analysing my body and noting how I can make it better both outside and in 6. Run for an hour while chanting incantations (as recommended by Anthony Robbins' 7-day program called *Get The Edge*) or do weights for thirty minutes and skipping rope for another 7. Make and have breakfast (freshly made vegetable juice, soy milk, two glasses of water with lemon squeezed on top, eight egg whites, oats mixed with almonds, two apples, one banana, sometimes some chicken from the night before) 8. Shower and get ready 9. Scan over my to-do list 10. Head to work (unless it's a Saturday; on Saturdays I stay at home and analyse my business and investments objectively and see where I'm heading and how I can improve them).

This book my mentor once encouraged me to read called *The Seven Habits of Highly Effective People* suggested that actively learning and staying consistent with the right habits is vital to any kind of success in life – that's why habits can either make or break you. I don't ever, ever want to become broken. Life gives no reward to broken people.

Things were different that morning. I woke up startled – I looked at my clock: it was already five. I hurriedly showered, shaved, ate breakfast. I sped to my office and ran three major orders that I was supposed to do before heading to bed. I answered a number of emails and made contact with my employees in India, and, for the first time, I apologised to one of them for not replying to one of their queries on time. It was a strange feeling, having extra sleep. I felt more tired, more restless, incredibly guilty. Even so, I couldn't help but keep looking at my mobile phone. Eventually, when I received no messages by noon I picked it up and dialled a number I'd been glancing at all day and walked outside.

"Hello?"

"Hey," I said.

"Hey, you." Kitty said in a chirpy voice. It sounded like she was outside.

"What are you up to?"

"I'm just sitting, having tea, eating lunch."

"Really? Sounds like a waste of time." I pictured her with a green tea and a shopping bag and my uncle in front of her, wondering who she was on the phone with. "I won't disturb you then."

"No, that's fine," she said. "I'm eating alone. And it's not a waste of time."

I grinned a little. "You like eating alone, don't you?"

She giggled. "I love being alone. Being alone gives me the chance to catch up with my thoughts."

"I'm impressed," I said. "I've always pictured you as the type who couldn't live without people by you all the time."

"People think that, but I'm actually a closet introvert."

"I'd never seen anyone ever say anything so positive about loneliness before. And about wasting time. And about being an introvert."

"The world needs more positivity."

I smiled. "It certainly does. Take Anthony Robbins, for instance. He always talks about how positive people should be, and look how successful he is now."

"Who's Anthony Robbins?"

I stopped walking. "Are you serious?"

"Should I know him?"

After holding back my anger and calmly telling her that Anthony Robbins was the most inspiring person in the world, we spoke for a while longer until we reached a silence, and in that gap of silence I suddenly realised that I'd been walking around in circles for the past thirty minutes. I looked back at my office, which I also used as a warehouse for my stock. "Listen," I told her. "I have to go."

After work I took a protein shake and an energy booster before heading to the twenty-four hour gym I was a member of and regularly supplied my products to. I did about fifteen minutes of dynamic stretches and talked to a few of the regulars about our recent workouts and the best kinds of protein to use. I then went on the treadmill for about twenty minutes, running on speed 14 and listening to an audio book of Robert Kiyosaki's *Secrets of the Rich*. I then focused purely on my biceps: I did numerous combinations of super sets involving dumbbell curls, concentration curls and incline curls. Afterwards I walked around, starting friendly conversations with people in the gym. I flirted with a wealthy looking girl who was new there and, using similar sales strategies I'd learnt and used before (push pull, understanding needs and egos, asking open-ended questions, ethos, pathos, logos), built up her interest in my business. I gave her my business card, completely confident that she'd eventually buy one of my products and refer me to her friends and possibly even her potentially wealthy family. I said goodbye and went into the bathroom, where I looked at myself at different angles while subtly comparing the tone of my body and the size of my penis to the other guys in the bathroom. I took a bath, put on new clothes, looked at myself at different angles again. I considered taking a photo of myself but then changed my mind.

I took another protein shake before heading to my car. I checked my mobile messages: there were a few business emails, there was a text from my sister, there was a text from my uncle, there was a text from Kitty. I read the text from Kitty and drove to her apartment and spent the evening watching DVDs with her. I hadn't watched a movie in a long time, and seeing them reminded me of when I was about seven years old and my mum bought me a VHS of the original Superman movie. I watched it for fifteen days straight. What a waste of time.

I reached home at midnight. I received a call from the girl in the gym and flirted with her while constantly checking the time on my watch. The time was worth it, because I eventually sold her and a friend some of my product over the phone, guaranteeing myself more passive income for the next 12 months. After cutting my other bicep for arriving home late again I lay on my bed and turned over, and then turned over again, and then turned over again repeatedly.

I woke up at four in the morning and groaned. I was one hour behind schedule and both my biceps were stinging. I opened my window but had no time to meditate or write my goals in life. I headed to the kitchen to prepare breakfast. I turned on the news. I opened my fridge – I'd forgotten to buy egg whites, so I settled with oats, almonds, tuna pasta, as well as a bowl of two sliced apples and bananas mixed with yoghurt and sprinkled with trail mix. I ate a piece of Lindt chocolate Kitty gave me the night before and considered spitting it out, but didn't.

When I have my first son the story I'll tell him again and again will be about my first hundred thousand dollars. I used to be an ugly bastard, you see, and I was stupid: I was never the popular kid in class and I never really achieved anything and nobody ever really placed their hopes in me. One day I woke up and realised how hungry I was. I was physically hungry, but I was also hungry for other things. I wanted to be as happy as the people I'd see on TV. I wanted to not be limited by money. I wanted women to lust after me. I wanted friends to appreciate me. I wanted to stop feeling weak. Most importantly, I wanted to be able to give my siblings a life that my parents never could.

I realised that I'd been doing it all wrong: I'd been feeling sorry for myself too much and blaming other people too much and preventing myself from really achieving anything in life. I realised that to be wealthy, I had to do exactly what wealthy people did – we all have twenty-four hours in a day and we all have enormous challenges; it's *how* we spend these twenty-four hours and how we overcome these enormous challenges that separate us from the rest. I had to not desire alcohol. I had to not desire cigarettes. I had to stop complaining and start thinking optimistically about everything. I had to attend seminars and read books on business, negotiation, NLP, dating, public speaking. I found a shitty job and I invested whatever shitty money I was paid into seminars and books and my business and my gym membership. My sisters yelled at me to study and to choose a normal life; my workmates gave me shit for doing what I did. I doubted myself so often that I'd cry like a little girl and scream and sob into my pillow before sleeping for two or three hours, only to wake up again to work even more. I was in enormous debt and nobody loved me and I didn't love myself.

I was an absolute embarrassment, but one day I realised that I was making a thousand dollars a month from my endeavours. One day I realised that I was making a thousand dollars a week from my endeavours. One day I realised that I was making a thousand dollars a day from my endeavours. One day I realised that I was making a thousand dollars an hour from my endeavours, and I was making it all without the need for investors or loans or full time employees or other bullshit other business people need – I did it all on my own. I paid off my credit cards and bought seven hundred dollar sunglasses and a BMW and picked my sisters up from somewhere and we drove along the beach and I told them, I fucking told you so.

Anyway that was a story for the future. My real concerns that day were to do with marketing. I had to look over and revise my marketing plan: I had to significantly improve my television advertising, radio advertising and digital marketing if I wanted to achieve at least forty percent growth that year. I'd outsourced a local company to improve my company's website search engine optimisation to ensure that when people searched for health and fitness equipment on Google, they'd find my website first and be encouraged to purchase my products. The company I hired for the job was doing shit work and my contact was barely replying to my emails. By then I'd normally be yelling at them over the phone, but that time, for some reason, I didn't care so much. My mind was on the movies I watched with Kitty and the expression on her face when she asked me if I wanted to stay over as it was "pretty late already" and that I "might be too tired to drive home". I looked down and told her that I was driving home because my bed was there and that was it.

As I clicked around the programs open on my computer screen I received a phone call.

"Hey, man." It was my uncle.

"Hey," I said, wishing that I hadn't answered my phone. I could hear music and some of his friends joking around in the background. "What are you guys up to?"

"We're just drinking before going to the casino. Want to come?"

"Nope," I said. "It's ten in the morning by the way."

"You're boring, you're like, you're really boring for a kid."

"I've always been boring."

"Nah, man," he slurred, "I remember, I remember one time once. You said… a joke."

"Yeah? What joke?"

"Fuck I don't remember. You were like eight years old and you said some shit about a sausage roll." He chuckled.

"Oh yeah," I said as I logged out of a website and minimised a screen. "I remember that joke. I said it all the time."

"How'd it go again?"

"How do you make a sausage roll?" I started.

"How?"

"Push it."

My uncle didn't laugh. "I remember now."

"I can't believe you just made me say a stupid joke."

"I'm drunk," he said.

"What's new?"

"Shut up."

I was slightly worried about asking this, but: "Anyway, what the hell did you call me for?"

"Nothing, man, just wanted to see how you were. If you were still being a loser with no social life."

"If by being a loser you mean being successful, fit, good looking and having a Mercedes-Benz SLK in my garage, then my answer is yes, I'm still a loser."

"You know, I can't believe you moved out so soon, you know? Your sisters and I, we missed you so much, we missed you so much. And then you started a trend or something, because they all started moving out after you." My uncle yelled something to one of his friends in the background before concentrating on our conversation again. "Sorry, Harry was being a total cunt about some guy's car we axed last night. Anyway, have you heard from Kitty?"

"You axed someone's car?"

"I don't know, man. Have you heard from Kitty?"

"Not really, what's up?"

"Nothing. I finally spoke to her the other afternoon and we hooked up a bit but I haven't heard from her at all since then."

"Really? Hooked up?" I cleared my throat. "Like, what do you mean, *hooked up*?"

"Just hooking up, man," my uncle said. "Like making out. I touched, I touched her tits and shit. Anyway, so you haven't heard from her at all?"

"I think she texted me but I don't really remember," I mumbled.

"Anyway, fuck, whatever. I'm going to win ten thousand bucks tonight."

"Sure you will, you dumb bastard," I said. By then I'd put my phone on speaker and was flicking through all of Kitty's text messages. Which afternoon did she see my uncle? When did she have the time? Maybe it was the afternoon before I came over his place. But wouldn't he have told me then?

"I will, and you'll realise money should be easily made. It shouldn't be earned by waking up at three in the morning every morning."

"It's not the reward, but the journey. It's the power of habit."

"Bullshit." He hung up.

I stared at my screen and scrolled up and down some documents without really thinking about what I was looking at or why I was scrolling up and down some documents. I started writing an email to my dick of a contact at the search engine optimisation company that was supposed to help my business but then spent half an hour typing and deleting and typing the same message over and over again.

I walked out of my office and called Kitty.

"Why hello there."

"Hey, kid," I started.

"You do know I'm older than you, right?"

"Doesn't matter," I said. "You're still a kid in my eyes."

She laughed. "How's life? Did you start reading that book I told you about?"

For a moment, I had no idea what she was talking about. Then suddenly: "*The Alchemist*?"

"You haven't started reading it, have you?"

"I'd be lying to your face if I say I have."

She giggled. "You'd lie to my face? You're a terrible person."

"I'm only terrible on the surface. If you peel back the layers, I'm actually a really good guy."

"You have to read it," she said. "It's one of the most beautiful books I've ever read."

"It looks like new age bullshit," I complained.

"It's not."

"I've always been more into business books," I said as I crossed the street and smiled and nodded at a guy I recognised from the gym. "They help people contribute more to society. I find that all fiction books do is make people dream, but that's it. They fantasise but don't create fantasies. It's for lazy people who want nothing more than to escape from reality as easily as possible without any effort whatsoever."

"What's wrong with that? You're an action man, but not everyone wants to be an action man," she said, completely missing the point. "Plus, fiction can do things to a person that nothing else can. They help us realise bits about people and things that we never would've observed before. Plus, they help us emphathise more with others than what self-serving business books do."

"Sure." I wasn't interested. What I was really interested in was what happened between her and my uncle.

"One day, you'll understand."

"We'll have to see about that."

"Speaking of business books, I've almost finished *Think and Grow Rich*."

"Really?" I glanced at a café, considered buying a green tea to calm myself down, but didn't. "What do you think of it?"

"I mean, yeah, it's inspirational. The first two chapters are like, pretty motivational, and I can see why you enjoy business books. I never thought about Ford as Henry Ford. I thought the word Ford just represented boring cars."

"Ford was one of the greatest business people of all time, and the first two chapters of Think *and Grow Rich* were the greatest chapters of any book I've ever read in my entire life."

She laughed at that, but I don't know why. "The chapter on sexual transmutation is kind of weird."

"It makes sense, if you think about it."

"It's just weird."

That annoyed me, but I didn't tell her that. "Anyway it's a good book. Right now, when I can, I'm reading Peter Lynch's *One Up On Wall Street*. You should totally read it too if you want to take your investments seriously."

"Sounds dull already," she giggled. "Let me guess, it's written by an old guy in a suit?"

"Yeah it is but it's nothing but dull. It's about investing in stocks as actual investors, not get-rich-quick traders who are nothing but gamblers. I mean, this guy, he invested in Apple shares when they were just about five bucks. You know how much money he'd have by now?"

"Life isn't always about money."

I found a ledge and sat down on it. "Money is important because it leads to progress."

"You can achieve progress without money," Kitty said.

"How?"

"You just can," she said.

"Money creates jobs. Money creates hospitals. Money creates charities."

"Money also creates monsters. Plus, it's not the money that creates these jobs and these hospitals or whatever," Kitty said. "It's the people behind the money. What we're lacking is not people who are driven to make money, but people who are driven to help change the world for the better. We've all structured our lives in a way that prioritises the need for money... and it's sad, because there are all these geniuses in the world, all these really smart, hardworking people, wasting their lives to pay their bills instead of investing their time to find ways to improve the way everyone lives. And I have to admit, I'm not doing any better. I'm just sitting here, drinking tea instead of making a difference. But at least I'm aware of this, and I know one day I'll get my act together."

"Is that so?" In the distance, I could see my gym. The sign said *Absolute Absolute Fitness*, and to the right of those words were giant silhouettes of a man doing a dumbbell curl and a big-titted woman jumping over a skipping rope.

Kitty and I spoke for about an hour. Throughout that hour I should've gone back to work, but I didn't – I kept sitting on that ledge and I kept speaking to her. I don't know why. I wasn't sure if it even made me happy – it certainly didn't make me sad. In the end, I decided not to ask her if she'd met up with my uncle recently.

The first time I gambled was in primary school. I was waiting for my turn to play handball, and I turned to this kid next to me and said that I bet three bucks that Alan, the Chinese guy, would win. He said sure. In the end I lost three bucks. Angry, I bet that Jeff, the redhead kid with a bit of a temper, would make it to King. I lost again. I kept losing. For weeks. Everyone made fun of me and I hated them for thinking that I could lose at something. I never gambled again. Unless, of course, if you call running an extremely profitable high-growth enterprise gambling. But then you'd be an idiot if you did.

I walked back to my office, checked my phone messages and checked my email inbox. I sat there, clicking the mouse blankly. When I realised that I'd been daydreaming I angrily pulled a notepad out and wrote down, *Don't be a bullshit. You must work. Every day in every way you're getting better and better, wealthier and wealthier. More money must come in.* I then wrote down what needed to be done for the day, but by then I'd slacked off on so much that it all seemed like a complete hassle. I leant back and sighed. Where did my focus go?

I received a text from Kitty: *There's a new café I want to try. Want to head there after dinner tonight? Your shout :P* I replied with, *Yeah, sure.* I shut my computer down and headed to the gym.

That night, I took Kitty to a restaurant that my mentor told me about that was located right near the river.

The last time I'd ever been to a restaurant as fancy as that was a year ago, when it was my sister's birthday and I treated my whole family to dinner and a live showing of *Cats*. I paid ten thousand dollars for that evening and I secretly wished everyone knew that I paid ten fucking thousand dollars for that evening.

Anyway, the bottom line is that Kitty and I were in the most expensive and most well reviewed restaurant in the city, and it was all possible because of my successes. The room was grand, the plates were grand, the chandelier was grand, the cars outside were grand, the windows were grand. Everyone looked like they were about five thousand years old.

Kitty looked around at everything and then looked at me: I was wearing a suit. "I kind of went over the top tonight, didn't I?" I grinned.

She laughed. "You think?" I looked at her and at the way she dressed and put on her makeup. She presented herself differently and a little more elegantly than usual, but definitely not different and elegant enough – it was my fault: I told her that I was going to take her to somewhere fancy, but not this fancy.

My phone vibrated and I looked at it – my uncle was calling. I put the phone back into my pocket and ordered a twelve-course degustation meal for the both of us. Things kept coming, things that I didn't care much about but tasted pretty fucking good anyway. When I was a kid I assumed that good food meant a meat pie, or a microwave pizza, or some mince and potatoes and chopped vegetables, or, if my sisters and I were lucky, Sizzlers, or McDonald's, or my favourite: KFC. I didn't know that good food could also mean about twenty different chefs with years of experience, fresh ingredients, raw meat, giant chandeliers, an incredibly knowledgeable and friendly waiter, decade old wine and a gigantic bill.

I was afraid that Kitty would ask me if we were having a date, but she didn't, which was good and terrible at the same time. She looked at my watch. "That's a nice watch."

"Thanks," I said. "It was a gift from someone very special."

"Oh, from who?"

"From myself."

We both laughed. I didn't mention the fact that it was pretty obvious that my uncle's watch looked (and was) much more expensive than mine. I knew nothing much about watches and didn't care much for them, but no one ever gets that. The only brands I really know are Seiko and Rolex. I could've bought a watch for ten dollars for all I cared, but my mentor said that a good, expensive watch was a constant reminder of what I'd been able to accomplish so far and what I'll be able to accomplish in the future. It also helped obtain more clients – people love clinging onto success. My uncle, who knew a guy who knew a guy who sold non-imitation branded watches for cheap, helped me get my first Rolex. It looked larger than any other watch I'd seen. It shone brightly, and as I played with it in my hands I could tell that when it was made, people truly cared about the product they were making; they cared about the quality, about the profitability, about the brand, about who would be seen wearing it; a whole team would've dedicated a significant portion of their lives just to create this little gadget that could tell the time. I wondered if my real father ever dreamt of wearing watches as ridiculous as mine.

We finished eating and drinking and talking about nothing special and I paid the bill and we walked around for a while, talking about even more things that didn't help me achieve more success or wealth in life whatsoever. We then headed for my Mercedes and sat inside it and looked at each other, saying nothing and smiling slightly until we both sort of shyly laughed and didn't say why we both sort of shyly laughed. I turned the engine on and we drove to the café she wanted to try. It was east of the city, and they had the strangest flavoured coffees on the menu I'd ever seen. Like kiwi flavoured coffees, chilli flavoured coffees, beach flavoured coffees, bullshit flavoured coffees, I don't know. But whatever they were doing, they were doing okay. There were customers everywhere. I counted the staff and the equipment and the lighting and after some quick calculations in my head I concluded that it could have well been profitable, but not by much. I wondered how aggressive they were with their marketing, or if the novelty of the shit they were selling was all mainly from word-of-mouth.

I didn't drink coffee so I ordered a green tea.

"You're so boring," Kitty said. "We're in a place that specialises in coffee, and you're drinking tea?"

"I'm going to live longer than you," I said.

She giggled. "I'd rather burn out than fade out."

"I'd rather live a long life knowing that I changed the world for the better."

"By selling gym equipment?"

"By improving everyone's lives by supplying their gyms with only the best quality health machinery and tools and by providing homes with premium quality nutritional products." My phone vibrated and I looked at it: it was my uncle again. He'd been ringing the whole night.

"Sorry," I told Kitty, "I have to get this one." I answered my phone.

"Hello?"

"Where the fuck are you?" It sounded like my uncle had me on speaker phone – he was driving. "I was ringing your doorbell for fuckin' ages."

I looked at Kitty, stood up and walked outside of the café. "I'm out."

"Me too," he said. "I'll pick you up. Let's have a night out like we used to."

"I'm kind of busy with a potential client."

"You're always so fucking busy with a potential client," he said. "I'm heartbroken. Kitty has been ignoring me again. She hasn't been answering her phone. Help me."

"You don't need my help."

"You're right. But I haven't seen you in ages."

"You saw me a few days ago you stupid dumb fuck," I said.

"I'm bored, man. And Kitty is pissing me off. I need to talk to you."

"Stop being a bitch," I said.

"I fucking raised you."

"Tomorrow night?"

"Fine."

He hung up and I joined Kitty again.

"Who was that?"

"Some guy."

"Some guy?" She asked.

"You sound like a jealous girlfriend."

She giggled. "You wish."

I placed my napkin on my lap and faced Kitty and smiled. She was beautiful, sure, and I could understand why many men would desire her. But she could've been even better looking if she wasn't so damn lazy and unambitious. Firstly, she could've had smaller thighs and healthier skin and a straighter back. If she'd taken wheat grass as I repeatedly told her to, she would've had more vitality in her movements, making her even more attractive. Nothing turns me off more than a girl who doesn't mind eating cake in the evening, and Kitty was one of those girls who didn't mind eating cake in the evening. Look, the bottom line was this: she was a lazy person who'd had it easy all of her life and it'd affected her health and her looks. But I was worse, because I still sat there, still wanting to talk to her and call her and text her.

After coffee she mumbled that we should maybe hang out at my place for a while as she'd never seen it before. I didn't question her. We drove away from the café in silence; once in a while she'd glance at me and smile and once in a while I'd glance at her and smile.

We entered my home and I proudly showed her my gigantic TVs and my gigantic furniture and my gigantic collection of business books and sports trophies. I was happy, because she seemed genuinely impressed by all of them. After a while we ended up in my room, and as we sat on the edge of my bed, we kissed. As we kissed I remembered a book I once ordered online called *She Comes First: The Thinking Man's Guide to Pleasuring a Woman* and strategised where I should place my hands, and as I ran my hands down her body I made sure to consider the pace at which I should run my right hand towards her crotch area, and as I ran my right hand from her ankle to her knee then through her dress and up to her groin I suddenly thought about what time I had to wake up the next day, about the marketing I had to do, about the goals I set for the month, and then all of a sudden, out of nowhere, a few very important questions flickered through my mind: Would she still look as good as she does five years from now? Would she still look as good as she does ten years from now? Would she still look as good as she does when she's forty, forty plus? Should I ever even get married? Why didn't she comment on my abs? How come one of my suppliers didn't reply to my latest email?

"Keep sucking my nipples," she kept saying. So I did.

One of the first books I'd ever read about relationships was *The Game*, by Neil Strauss. Neil Strauss was a balding writer (a loser) who rarely had any kind of successes with women until he met this guy who called himself Mystery. Mystery claimed that he was a modern day Casanova – like Neil, he started off as an ambitious loner who, after a lot of hard work, turned himself into a natural "player" who was able to have sex with hundreds of beautiful women. Anyway Neil, who ended up being one of the most respected players in the world of wannabe players, basically said that any man could get any woman because seduction, like life and achieving any sort of success in life, was all a game – all they needed to know was how to press the right buttons. If only my father had read *The Game*. If only he knew what women wanted. If only he didn't leave us behind.

I woke up next to Kitty at six in the morning. I hurriedly showered and ate a piece of toast and a boiled egg and kept hoping that she wouldn't be there when I returned to my room, that it was all some kind of sick dream. But she was there, she was right where I left her. I leant forward and kissed her cheek and she smiled and looked up at me: it was strange; she looked better without her makeup.

"Wake up."

She smiled. "Time for me to go?"

"I've got places to go, people to see."

I handed her a piece of toast and after we spoke for a few minutes, she brushed her teeth and left. I sent a few emails with my phone and drove as quickly as I could to meet my mentor. As I didn't have time to recite my incantations out loud in the morning I decided to do them while driving: *I will be a symbol of true success day in, day out! I will be a glowing being of pure integrity and wealth! I will build an empire that will bring me shitloads of hard cash so that I can build schools in third world countries and leave a never-ending legacy for my children, my grandchildren and great grandchildren! I will never work for anyone and will only ever work for myself! I will never ever come back to the life that I used to live! I will not think about my awful lonely past, I refuse to! I will never be depressed again, I swear, I will never be fucking depressed again! Every day, in every way, I'm getting better and better, wealthier and wealthier... Life is good... Life is good... Life is good...*

I arrived at some restaurant in the Hilton to see my mentor, who was waiting at a reserved table. She tapped her watch and, although she was smiling, crossed her head disappointedly at me.

"I have no excuse," I smiled.

"I've got places to go, people to see," she said.

I sat down in front of her and picked up the menu. "You know what? I said that exact line to someone this morning."

"You always steal my lines."

"I'm pretty sure you didn't create that line," I said.

"I didn't create it, but I sure did copyright it."

"Stop trying to be funny," I said. "You're completely failing."

"I'm not the one who's laughing right now."

I looked around the room. "Can you see anyone laughing?"

"You were laughing just then."

"Do you have proof of that, bitch?"

"I don't need proof, buddy," she said. "And you can stop looking at the menu. I've ordered your food."

"I'd say thanks, but you always order the worst tasting vegan shit in the world."

"I thought you loved eating shit."

"That's where you're wrong. I love quality food, which I can never seem to get when I'm out with you."

My mentor started her life with three dollars. She ran away from her home with her boyfriend who got her pregnant and ended up leaving her for another man. To make enough money for her and her child, she tried selling drugs for a while and even sold her body once or twice. Eventually, she was hired by a kind and patient fat woman who ran a bakery and ended up being like a mother to her. One day a customer told my mentor about this "network marketing" program (or "pyramid scheme" as I always tell her) that helped him achieve twenty thousand dollars a month in passive income through the buying and selling of cleaning products. She joined the pyramid scheme and soon enough, she was also earning twenty thousand dollars a month in passive income. She invested everything she earnt from that into real estate, stocks and her own company: a Supreme Lifestyle Coaching company that helps people achieve their dreams, plus more. Now she has books, audio books, eBooks, DVDs, YouTube videos, podcasts, magazine articles and a whole heap of other bullshit that keeps making her even more money. She hosts seminars all over the world; she has "Billionaire Maker Teams"; she runs three day "Unlimited Super Wealth and Extreme Success" bootcamps that hundreds of attendees willingly pay twelve thousand dollars each to attend. Her goal is to achieve fifteen million dollars a month in passive income. She is incredibly sexy, yet incredibly intimidating – she's the type of woman men always look at but never dare approach.

I first met her during one of her seminars and realised that she was the perfect stepping stone for me to get where I wanted to be. I approached her right afterwards and told her that I wanted her to be my mentor. At first, she said that she didn't have time for another protégé, but I kept calling her, emailing her, abusing her staff. Eventually she gave in and said that I needed to pay her twenty five thousand dollars per one hour meeting for it to work out, but I said that I'm only paying five thousand dollars per two hour meeting – we settled at fifteen thousand dollars per one and a half hour meeting.

My mentor looked me up and down. "You're getting a little haggard. What's wrong, pussing out from the stresses of life?"

"I have a dilemma," I said.

"It's a girl, isn't it?" she said.

"It's always about a girl."

"Successful people get girlfriends, wives and even *families*, yet they don't look half as tired as you do. What on earth did she do to you?"

"Could this just be an adjustment period?" I asked her. "When people start relationships, they usually get a little lazy with everything, don't they?"

"Well if it is an adjustment period, you have to make it fly by as quickly as possible."

"How the hell do you do that?" I asked her, kind of knowing what she was going to tell me.

"You either break up with them, or you go back to your goals and read them out loud and you snap back into the routine that was bringing you the successes you were achieving before you met her; however, since you don't want to ignore your relationship, you have to find the perfect balance of a profitable routine and a profitable relationship. Then, once you get to know each other more, you leverage each other's strengths to further benefit your successes further. But if she keeps distracting you from your goals, if she's not willing to support a hardworking man who wants to make a difference in this world, then she's not the right girl for you."

"How about you?" I asked, completely not interested in what she just said. "Do you have a man now?"

"I do and it's great," she said. "But we're talking about you today, dear. Did you bring your financial reports?"

"Sure did." I pulled the documents out of my bag and handed them to her. She scanned them over quickly before nodding. "You seem to be doing okay, but I'll show this to my accountant first. How was the search company you employed?"

"They're shit," I said.

"That's why you have to use mine."

"The people you recommend to me are always expensive."

"You get what you pay for. Trust me, you'll enjoy the profitability these guys will bring to your table. They've worked wonders for my companies."

"You say that because you get a cut every time you recommend someone to them."

"So what if I am? They're the exact same people I use, and I know they're great."

"Fine," I said. "Send me their number after breakfast."

"Have you looked into new properties like I told you to?"

I sighed. "Didn't I tell you that it's a waste of time? That real estate just isn't my thing?"

"You told me to go fuck myself," she reminded me.

"And did you?" I grinned.

"I don't know why I put up with you. You're

nothing," she said. "You're smaller than a grain of dust."

"I'll be something one day. I'll probably be even wealthier than you are right now."

"If you truly want to be something, if you really want to get better at me at this game, then follow my advice. Even if just for tax reasons." She poured some sugar in her tea and stirred it vigorously. "Look, you're paying me money for my advice, and my advice is for you to buy more properties with all this extra cash you're making. It'll help offset all that tax you're paying. I've even given you the precise locations to buy in, what kind of trust and company structures you should form with your accountants and which agents and solicitors to call. I've made life incredibly easy for you. You know how much advice I had when I started? None."

"Can't you just do it all for me?"

"Don't even start with that, you little shit," she said. "It's your job to buy property. Property means land. Land is rare. You need land. You need to own what's rare in this world."

"Don't be stupid. There's land everywhere."

She gave me the finger. "Fuck you."

The waitress arrived with our food. We both looked up at her and smiled. "Thank you."

"You're very welcome," she smiled back.

I looked back at my mentor. "Fine, I'll think about getting a property," I lied. "Have your PA email me what I need to do."

"Don't just think about it, honey. Do it."

"How's your PA doing anyway? Has he filed a sexual harassment case against you yet?"

"Very funny," she said. "He's still fine and he's still very good looking. Much better looking than you will ever be."

"That's because he's gay," I said.

"Whatever. Now tell me about this girl."

I took a bite out of my food, which was made out of what looked like egg and a whole lot of other expensive looking shit. "She's just a girl."

"What makes her a better girl than other girls?"

I thought about her for a second. I thought about the very first time I met her: she was on my uncle's couch, reading some kind of depressing looking book that had nothing to do with personal development. She had jeans and a tight-fitting t-shirt and a lot of makeup on and her hair was tied up and her eyebrows looked nice and she peered out of her book to smile at me. I shrugged. "To be honest, I really don't know. She's kind of a lazy person."

She leant towards me. "Does she encourage you to become more successful?"

"She obviously doesn't."

"Is she pretty?"

"She's okay."

"Does she make you happy?"

"Stop asking me so many questions."

"You're such a cute little boy." My mentor laughed and pinched me on the cheek before I slapped her hand away. "You're blushing! What kind of girl will make you blush and look so stressed out?"

"I'm not blushing and I'm not stressed out."

"Wait a minute. I know what type of girl she is," she said. "Please, please tell me I'm wrong."

"What? Tell me what type of girl she is, you fucking smart arse."

"You ready?"

"I'm not, actually. You look fucking creepy right now."

"She's a taken girl," she concluded proudly, as if she was some detective who had uncovered some big secret. "She's taken," she repeated, just to make sure I heard what she said all over again.

I didn't say anything, so she crossed her head.

"I knew it. You're such a *guy*. A guy with a stupid penis. This is why I don't believe in the ritual of marriage – there are just no good men out there." She pointed at me with her fork while crossing her head even more. "No, no, no. You can't do this, you bastard. Any form of cheating will lead to destruction. Trust me on that one."

"So you're saying there's scientific evidence out there that proves that every single person who has and who ever will cheat will live a life full of destruction? Show me. Show me that fucking evidence."

"Don't be smart. From my experiences and from the experiences of hundreds of people I've met during my seminars… I can confidently say that anyone who's unfaithful or causes someone to be unfaithful will suffer terrible consequences. There will always be terrible, terrible consequences."

I snickered. "'*Terrible consequences*'? Look at you. You fucking, you fucking sound like one of those crazy fortune tellers in the movies. Listen, neither of us is cheating. I'm certainly not cheating. It's just… it's just a bit complicated, okay?"

My mentor kept nagging me about it some more until I convinced her to shut up and give me more advice about business. After another hour of going over some strategies with me, I paid the bill and told her that I'll transfer her the money for her time and she smiled and said thanks. As we walked to her new Porsche she told me, "Listen, life is about maintaining a balance of positive and negative consequences. You can never have too much positivity and you can never have too much negativity. If you decide to tip towards one direction of the seesaw too much, everything on the other side will spill on top of you and it will destroy you. Don't you get it? Don't fuck up, okay?" and I told her to shut up about the metaphors and she kissed me on the cheek and I watched her drive off.

What's your definition of a successful investor? was what someone asked a presenter in one of the hundred or so seminars I went to when wanting to become successful. The speaker said this: a successful investor is someone who lives off passive income, which is income that arrives in your bank account without you having to actively work for it. He or she doesn't work as an employee; instead, the successful investor employs a team of highly talented people who help his or her wealth grow. A successful investor is a person who travels overseas three or four months at a time and also invests in those countries. The successful investor loves to invest in undervalued stocks, or properties, or businesses, or scripts, or people – they love to see beauty in things that other people do not, and then profit tremendously from it when the rest of the world finally catches on. I believed he was full of shit. To me, a successful investor is someone who has amassed a billion dollars in cash in their bank account and that's about it.

My uncle called me on the drive to my office. He didn't sound like himself. "We need to talk."

"About what?" I asked him, knowing exactly what he wanted to talk about.

"About Kitty. Just come over," he said. "I've been trying to see you for so long. You better not cancel on me tonight because I have a bone to pick with you."

"Who the fuck says 'I have a bone to pick with you' nowadays?"

"I do."

"Good for you," I said. "I kind of have a lot of work to catch up on."

"Remember when you said family is number one? Just fucking come over."

"Fine," I said. "But I can only stay for about an hour."

I arrived at his house and he was standing on the driveway, arms akimbo, waiting for me. He looked like he'd aged five years: his hair was all over the place and there were deep, dark craters under his eyes.

"You look like shit," he said.

"So do you."

We stood there, just staring at each other, until he suddenly grinned and hugged me. "Long time no see, you fucker."

"It's been about three days."

"Three days is too long."

"Really? How much of a pussy are you?"

We went inside and the house had no one else in it, which was strange for a Friday. "Where's Danny?" I asked him.

"He's out."

"How about Bill?"

"He's out with Danny," my uncle said.

I looked around, both hoping and not hoping that at least one other person would be at home. "And Kieran and the rest of the boys?"

"They're out. Anyway why the fuck do you care? You never ask about those guys."

"I'm just asking," I said.

We sat down and my uncle gave me a beer and I said no, but he kept insisting I drink some so I ended up taking a bottle and having a few sips. As I drank I remembered the time my uncle showed my sisters and I his gun collection. "These are only a few of the guns that I can show you," he told us. There was a shotgun, a pistol, a revolver and what looked like a sniper rifle. I wanted to ask him if he'd ever shot anyone before, but for some reason I could never push the question out of my mouth.

My uncle slapped my knee. "So, what have you been up to?"

I shrugged. "Just working, man."

"Just working, man?"

"Yeah, just working, man."

"Nothing else?"

"Nothing else," I said, the image of my uncle's gun collection blaring into my mind. "Stop interrogating me."

"Have you seen Kitty?" he finally asked me. "I mean, you mentioned that she texted you the other day right?"

"I haven't seen her," I quickly said. I glanced at the exit of the house. I quickly looked at my uncle's pants, at his pockets, at what was next to him: he didn't seem to have a gun with him. But if I had to run out of there, I still had to pass through my uncle first. But I was fitter than he was; maybe I could kick his head if he grabbed my legs. Once I knock him down, I could run for it and drive the hell out of there and leave the country or something. "Why?"

"Well, she tells me you guys have seen each other."

I looked up and pretended to struggle to find the memory of seeing her a few nights ago. "Oh yeah, we did. I leant her a book."

"Which book?" he asked me.

"*Think and Grow Rich*," I said.

"Haven't read it."

"Well," I glanced at the door again, "you should if you want to be wealthier than you are now."

"Why didn't you just tell me that you met her, that you hung out together?"

"I knew you were having issues with her, man, and I didn't want to piss you off."

My uncle put on an incredibly forced smile. "You knew I was having issues with her and you still wanted to see her? And you didn't even bother to tell me?"

"Like she rang me up," was the excuse I found myself suddenly coming up with. "She wanted to borrow the book. You know how she likes books, right? How she's always reading a book or talking about a book? One day, remember when we were all out having coffee, and you went out to the toilet? I told her about *Think and Grow Rich* and she kept asking if she could borrow it after that. She kept texting and calling me about it. I wanted to ignore her but she kept texting me. I'm really sorry, man, you know Kitty and I are okay friends and I didn't want to piss you off. It was nothing to me, so I thought it better not to tell you about her annoying me like that. I should've told you about it though, I know. I'm sorry, I really am." For some reason, I then added: "All we ended up doing was talk about her dramas with you anyway."

"Really now," he said, seeming to be impressed by my last line.

"Really," I complained. "She wouldn't shut up about you."

"So you met each other," my uncle said.

"Yeah," I replied. "She told you we met up, right?"

"I was just joking about that. I wanted to scare you."

I laughed, all of a sudden feeling incredibly hot. I thought about a bunch of men murdering Kitty, and then murdering me. "Oh, well, yeah, we didn't really *meet up*, meet up. I dropped by her place and handed her the book and we spoke in the hallway and that's about it."

"You went to her place? You actually know where she lives?"

I remembered the exact date I sent her a text message, asking her where she lived. "Well I didn't ask for it. She texted me her address and told me to meet her at her place. We just met in front, that's about it."

"Really? You spent a few hours, just talking in her apartment hallway?"

"It was pretty uncomfortable," I said. "But she just wanted to keep talking and talking about you."

"So you didn't go anywhere else," he asked flatly.

"Of course not."

My uncle pulled his phone out and scrolled through something. "So the photos she uploaded here on Facebook, the ones that have you and her in a café, they're all made up?"

I knew it. I knew I should've listened to my sisters and started a Facebook account. I clicked in the air, pretending that the memories were all coming back to me. "Shit, yeah, that's why I don't remember being that uncomfortable in the hallway. It's because we actually went out for a really short drive to the café that's right near her place. You know that café? She just wanted to let out all her issues about you, and she made me promise not to tell you any of it. That's right. And I was like, put in this really awkward position of being a trusted friend or telling you everything right away. I mean, like I was going to tell you everything in the end anyway. Fuck, she's going to kill me for telling you all of this... I know that you're more important than she is, but you know..."

My uncle put on a slight grin. "You know she didn't post anything on Facebook about you having coffee, right? That I just made this up?"

"Oh yeah?" I said, still trying to maintain a positive, jokey expression on my face even though deep inside my heart was exploding. I wanted to get the hell out of there. My uncle's fists were curled in tight balls; I'd never seen his knuckles so white before. "I figured that." I forced out another laugh. "Man, that's so funny that you guessed us having coffee together so accurately. As I said, I completely forgot we had coffee. I've just had so much on my mind lately. You've known me since I was born. You know how it is. Like, when I get focused on work so much

I forget everything else."

"So you forgot you had coffee three nights ago?"

"Of course. You're a business person. You know how many things go on in our heads. It was a really, really quick coffee and as I said, all she talked about was you. So like, stop interrogating me," I said, realising how fragile and afraid I sounded.

"Do you like her?"

"Who?"

"Do you like Kitty?"

There was a pause, before I said: "No, no, I know she's out of bounds. Of course not. I mean, don't get me wrong, she's good looking and all –"

"You think she's good looking? You've checked her out?"

"I mean, yeah, she okay. It's a compliment man; fuck, it means you have good taste, calm down."

"Calm down?" My uncle stared at me, and I forced myself to stare at him back innocently. As I stared at him I thought about a number of things: that I was a coward, that I was a terrible person, that I had to get out of there, that he looked much older than I did, that the lines all over his face were deep, that he raised my sisters and I even though he didn't have to, that Kitty might be in trouble, that I'd miss him if we were to fall apart, that I screwed up, that I didn't screw up, that I owed him my life for raising me. Fuck this.

All of a sudden my uncle grinned, then laughed. He slapped my shoulder, causing me to flinch. "Man," he said, "you should see how nervous you look right now. Why, are you scared of me?"

"Fuck you."

"I'm your uncle, your best friend."

"Whatever."

He kept laughing. "You lied so much to me just then!"

"I didn't. I didn't lie at all. I told you that I just forgot and that, you know, I was going to tell you everything anyway. I just promised her not to tell you anything, that's all."

He leant back against his couch and grinned. "I tell you this all the time. Don't ever be afraid of anything." That was the first time he'd ever told me that. "I don't want you to grow up being a coward. It's Kitty that's the problem, man. Things were fucked up between us, but as you said the other night, there are other women out there. Other women with bigger tits, right? Anyway, I was just kidding earlier: Kitty actually did tell me about how you guys had coffee and have been texting each other, and we had a long talk, and things are fine. And she told me that you probably didn't want to tell me about it yet to protect her, and that you knew how crazy I'd get. I just hadn't spoken to her properly like that in so long, you know? But we're both ready to move on. So if you want to go for her, go for her. I'll be happier if you didn't, but family is more important. Just be honest with me about this shit, okay? We all know that you're a shitty liar. I'm your uncle. You know you can never hide anything from me."

I looked at him, waiting for him to do something, but when he stayed there, relaxed, his arms draped around both sides of his couch, I also leant back against my seat and let out a relieved laugh. "So you're okay?"

"Yeah," my uncle said. "I'm okay. Why wouldn't I be, man?"

"You sure? Because I promise you there was nothing more to it besides that coffee and a few texts," I said.

"I'm sure. You're my favourite guy in the world. I won't let some bitch get in the way of that."

"I'm sorry I didn't tell you anything."

My uncle waved the idea away like it was already old news. "Tell me," he said, his smile dropping, "What's been up with you these past years, anyway?"

"What do you mean?" I asked him.

"What's been up with you?"

"I don't get you," I said.

"For the past few years, you've been all over the place. It's always us who has to call you. You've had this strange, serious look on your face since you've moved out and you've always been too busy for any of us. It's kind of hurtful, you know?"

"I don't know. I know that nobody understands this, and it'll be terrible if I lose you guys from my life, but I just really, really want to be successful. I'm addicted to it. I don't know why. I just need more money and I want things to be… perfect."

"Why aren't they perfect now?"

I'd only ever been bored once in my life. I was about nine years old and I was in my room, looking up at the ceiling, not knowing what to do. I sat up and stared at my toes and played with them for a little while. Then I walked around, constantly returning my attention to our house clock, hoping that it would be three o'clock in the afternoon. It was only ten in the morning. I was anxious.

Why couldn't I change time? What the hell was the point of having to wait for the three o'clock cartoons? Couldn't I have them right away? I called up the TV station and tried to get them to show the cartoons I wanted, but they didn't help me whatsoever. If only I knew about compound interest back then, if only I began investing…

The rest of my day was a productive one. I wrote emails, made calls, wrote plans. I did push-ups doing breaks. I turned my phone off. I decided that I'd completely forget about Kitty, that family was more important than some girl, that there was no point in asking her about her conversation with my uncle. I worked so hard that I ended up driving home at about eleven in the evening, after eating a late dinner on my own in the office (I had a fish steak with boiled broccoli, a green tea and three egg whites).

Things weren't so good when I reached my neighbourhood. As I approached my house I could see people standing around it, watching fire and smoke peacefully come out of its sides. It was a strange fire and it was strange smoke: it all seemed puffy, soft, innocent; it carefully went out then up to disappear in the sky. My neighbours were talking to each other and taking photos of the scene with their mobile phones. I reversed my car and stopped a few houses away. I rolled my window down and peered out and squinted at the scene. A fire truck arrived. A woman screamed. I checked my watch and thought about what I should do.

As I turned my engine back on and drove slowly past what was left of my home, I saw him: my uncle, standing there with his friends. He was wearing a shirt I'd never seen before – it was terribly white. He turned around and noticed me driving past: he nodded, scratched his nose with his middle finger, winked. I nodded back at him and kept driving.

As soon as I knew I was out of his sight I drove as quickly as I could towards Kitty's apartment. Why hadn't I checked on her earlier? I turned my mobile phone on and swore at it to hurry up and load. I checked my inbox: a few missed calls from her. I dialled her number but no one answered. I sped faster.

I'd only ever been scared once in my life. I was about fourteen years old. I saw my sister crying and I asked her what the hell was wrong – she pointed to the backyard outside. I walked to the window and saw my uncle with a few of his friends, laughing over some kids I recognised from school. They were all tied up. My uncle poured beer on them and his friends all laughed. My uncle and his friends began hurting them, and while they did my uncle turned around, noticed me, grinned and winked.

I parked on a garden somewhere and looked up: there was no fire. I ran to the apartment elevator. I repeatedly pressed the down button, waited for a thousand hours and rushed in as soon as the elevator door opened. I pressed the button for it to go up. As I walked back and forth inside the elevator a sudden thought came over me: Why don't I just drive away?

The elevator opened and I rushed out and quickly walked towards Kitty's door. I wiped my brow and before I reached it, I looked around: all I could find was a pot plant. I leant over, poured its contents out and picked it up. I could either smash it now and use a piece as a knife of some sort, or immediately throw it at someone's head if need be. I decided to keep it whole and immediately throw it at someone's head if need be.

I kicked her door and winced in pain as my foot rebounded, causing me to fall backwards onto the ground. "Kitty!" I yelled. I stood up and kicked it again and nothing happened again. I kicked it once more. Nothing happened, but someone from behind began opening the door. I got the pot ready.

"What are you doing?" Kitty looked at me, a shocked little expression plastered over her face as she opened the door. "Can you calm down?"

I looked at the pot in my hand, then at her. "Is everything okay?"

"Yes, why?" She giggled. "You should've told me you were coming here. I just showered and look like shit. Why haven't you been answering your phone all day? And why are you holding a pot? I swear, you're kind of weird sometimes."

Kitty's makeup was off and she had eye bags and her hair was all over the place. "You do kind of look like shit," I said.

"Shut up."

"So you're safe? Everything's okay?"

She shrugged. "Why wouldn't I be?"

"Just checking," I said.

"Want to put the pot down now?"

I looked at the pot and quickly put it down. "Uh, yeah. I saw it on the ground over there, that's all. Some idiot must've spilt your plant out." I pointed at its spilt contents around the corner.

"Oh really? That's terrible. I'll fix it up tomorrow. Want to come in?"

"That's okay."

"So you came here just to hold my pot and chat me up in the hallway?"

"Listen, why don't we run away?"

She smiled. "What, like in the books?"

"Like in the movies."

She smiled at this some more and leant against her doorway. "What do you think about me? Do you like me?"

"I never used to think negative thoughts until I met you."

"Is that some kind of twisted compliment?"

I scratched my head. "I really don't know what it is."

She moved forwards and placed her hands on my hips. "Have you ever heard the song called *Samson* by Regina Spektor?"

"Fuck no," I said. "Who the hell is that?"

"She's a singer. It's a beautiful song and I think it should be ours. Do you even listen to music?" She realised something. "Hang on, every time I've been to your car, there's never any music playing." She laughed and pointed at me. "You don't listen to music! You poor, poor child. Is there any creativity in you? Any creativity at all?"

I moved closer to her and tucked some hair behind her ear. She smelt good. "I just haven't found music that I like. Plus, I don't have time to listen to music. When the hell does someone have time to listen to music? All song lyrics are so depressing."

"When you drive, you idiot. When you work out. When you're sad. When you're in a club." She sighed. "I take it you haven't even been to a club. You're a businessperson. Business people need creativity to succeed, and music helps inspire that creative side. That's it. I'm making you your first mix CD."

I thought about what it would be like to listen to a music CD. That would mean I'd have to sacrifice some of the time I saved for listening to business audio books. "Well I guess Anthony Robbins listens to Aerosmith. And Steve Jobs listened to Bob Dylan. And they're both amazing people."

She touched my cheek. "You're cute."

"I'm not. I'm really not." I suddenly remembered why I was there. "But I'm serious. I think we have to leave. Tonight."

Kitty bit her lip, ignoring me. "I have to tell you something, and I think it has something to do with why you look so flustered right now."

"What is it?"

"I told your uncle that we had coffee with each other. I know I should've asked you about it first. But he kept bothering me, and you and I had this thing where we never mentioned him, not even once, and I don't know… I can't explain it, but I'm sorry. But don't worry. I never mentioned how… how intimate we've been, and about that night we had dinner together."

"Don't worry," I said. "I already know you told him. He asked me about it today."

"You're not mad?"

I thought about my burning home, about the fire and the neighbours and the smoke. "Why would I be?"

"Yeah," she smiled. "You shouldn't be. Your uncle is

a gentleman underneath. He took it very maturely, which was a surprise, even for me."

As I stood there with her a lot of bullshit thoughts rapidly passed through my mind. I thought about the first time I met her. I thought about her drinking from a cup of coffee with both of her hands. I thought about the first time I sent her a text message. I thought about her perfume, about her humungous dog. And then I thought about my mentor, about my bank balance, about my uncle grinning and giving me the finger. I didn't know what my thoughts were getting at, if they were even getting at anything at all. There had to be a book out there with a solution to my situation, but I had a feeling there wasn't. Maybe I should write one and turn it into a bestseller. I've never won at anything at life. It's like life created me for the sole purpose of turning me into a loser. But what life doesn't know is that one day I'm going to take revenge. I'm going to hurt it. I'm going to win at everything. At every single thing. I'm going to be president of the world. Im going to be emperor of the universe. I'm going to be made of gold and diamonds and deep inside, beneath my skin, beneath my layers, beneath my heart, beneath the barriers, you'll find my core, and that core will be made of toned muscle and perfection and you better be careful, you better tremble, because you won't want to look away. I hated Kitty. I wanted to hurt her. I wanted to split her in half with a samurai sword. I didn't want to let her go. I didn't want anything else or anyone else to have her. I wanted to take care of her, to give her an allowance and buy her a car and hold her shopping bags. With everything that happened that day I suddenly found myself in some kind of ugly tornado that I couldn't even begin to understand, and for some reason it felt good.

"Yes, he's a gentleman," I mumbled. "I don't know if you know anything about my uncle, but he doesn't let go of things so easily."

Kitty leant towards my left ear and whispered: "The worst is over, honey. Now come inside."

"I don't know," I said reluctantly, following her inside.

Eva, Part Three:
Fights and Fucking

There was one evening a few months into our relationship where I drove to Eva's friend's home (Eva'd been kicked out of her own home by her parents by then) and when I got there, late, she was waiting outside the front yard, smiling, wearing the shortest nightgown I'd seen in my life. We didn't have any money whatsoever and we never went out so we often just slept over each other's places or fought with each other or found something in the kitchen and ate together and talked about the world. She took my hand and walked me up to her room and sat me on the edge of her bed. She put some slutty music on and did this crazy dance in front of me. I tried my best not to laugh.

She asked me, *What do you want to be?* And I said, *A famous writer!* And then I asked her, *What do you want to be?* And she said the ruler of the world. She sat down next to me and we talked for hours.

When the morning came, we rummaged around my car for coins and drove to McDonald's and I bought her a shake and this cinnamon toast thing they had on special and we shared them both and kept talking even more. We drove to a university nearby and found an open field under the sunlight and we both took our clothes off and as I put her left ankle on my right shoulder she whispered something I couldn't hear.

We drove to my home and showered and changed. I told her to close her eyes as I placed a giant stuffed toy, a white bear, into her hands. She opened her eyes and squealed and hugged me. Afterwards Eva started working on some readings she had to do for one of her units and I walked to my computer and, unlit cigarette in my mouth, tried to write something. But I couldn't: out there, people were struggling, dying. But here I was, in love. What had I done to deserve someone like her? I'd done nothing.

Suicide After Break Up

I was drunk and I'd just finished another bout of crying and I didn't know how to kill myself properly so I searched it on Google. There were all sorts of websites and forums and opinions on how to do it, but in the end there was only one way to dramatically off myself that felt the most appealing: suicide by hanging. My plan was to hang myself in front of Jacob's place because all the shit that was happening in my world was his fault.

"It's true, it's true!" I cried to Jacob over the phone. "If you leave me, I'll kill myself!"

"I'm sick of this!" he yelled. "You threaten to do this every time we fight. I'm sick of your shit! Just die, Megan, I don't care!"

"I love you now. Isn't that enough?" And I hugged my pillow and curled into a ball and cried.

I drank another glass of something, wrote my suicide note, showered, put a cute skirt on, put some makeup on. I sent a few emo goodbye text messages to a few guy and girl friends as I straightened my hair and didn't respond to any of their replies or phone calls. As soon as I knew I was ready to die, I ran to my car and sped to Jacob's apartment complex.

I entered his apartment using unit keys he didn't

know I still had. I hadn't been in there in two months, and when I entered everything looked and smelt and felt normal again. I walked out to his unit's balcony and, looking down towards the ground that was quite far below, realised that I'd forgotten to bring rope or anything that I could've used to hang myself with. I checked the time on my phone: Jacob would probably be arriving from his morning gym session in five minutes.

I hurriedly looked around for something that I could create some sort of noose with. In the end I chose a blanket that Jacob and I used to cuddle under, back when we first started going out. It was sort of blue and faded, with little images of stars. *I like it when we kiss*, Jacob said and smiled when we were both underneath its warm darkness. I couldn't believe that Jacob still used it. I rolled it up and tied one end against a part of his balcony's balustrade, making sure to tie a triple knot. I then went to the other end and made a noose and fit it around my neck. I pulled.

"Shit," I coughed, quickly removing it when it felt too tight. It felt like a thumb pushing into my throat. I suddenly remembered something: my suicide note. I pulled it out of my bra, gave it one last read, rushed into the kitchen and put it on the bench and then rushed back out. I paused, wiped my nose, took a deep breath. I walked to the edge of the balcony again, but then I changed my mind and turned around and rushed back inside and found my mobile phone and called him. No one answered. I called him again and no one answered. I called him ten more times and no one answered. I texted him that I hated him, but there was no reply. I texted him that his friends told me some gossip about him, but there was no reply. I texted him that that I was so sorry to interfere with his precious day with a few calls and text messages, that he must have an amazing life now without me, and that this would be the last text that anyone in the world would ever get from me and that I love him and that I'm so sorry again and that he was pathetic and unforgiving. There was no reply. I texted him that I was actually going to die today, right outside his apartment, but there was no reply.

He should've been home half an hour ago.

All of a sudden, my phone vibrated. I checked who it was – it was Mum. I threw my phone against a wall and knelt on the ground and sobbed. I closed my eyes and ran my fingers over the cut marks all over my wrists and thighs; I thought about the time about a year ago when Jacob said I was gaining weight. I broke up with him; he spent a week trying to win me back. I walked over to the balcony again. I looked over the edge.

"I hate you this is selfish," I muttered, crying as loudly as I could. "I HATE YOU THIS IS SELFISH!"

I quickly put the noose around my neck again, tightened it and jumped off. The fall was short and full of fear and came to a painful halt as soon as the noose tightened around my throat. Although I wanted to scream, I couldn't. The pain and fear grew and grew and grew as I grabbed and clawed at the noose, trying to wiggle myself out of the stupid situation I'd brought myself into. I swung forwards and backwards, forwards and backwards, thinking about how I didn't want to die, thinking about how I wanted see Jacob at least once more, to even at least hold his hand. *Where are you? Why aren't you rescuing me?* I suddenly pictured a neighbour spotting me with an ugly expression on my face; I pictured my friends looking at a photo of my completely and utterly ugly self hanging from a balcony, my mouth limped open and eyes inflated, ready to pop, on some website online.

All of a sudden, I fell to the ground.

"Hhh…"

I spent some time desperately removing the noose and clinging onto my throat, coughing, gasping for air, before realising that there was an immense pain biting through my entire body – I'd fallen from pretty high up. I tried to scream in agony, but my voice felt like it'd gone forever. There was no blood anywhere but I felt like there should've been. I wondered how embarrassing the whole situation looked and why nobody bothered to help me. I looked up at the sheet that was dangling from the balcony: the noose mustn't have been tight enough. I lay there, gasping for air, feeling sorry for myself for a while before standing up and looking at the driveway. Where was Jacob? I sobbed.

I limped back into Jacob's apartment and dusted myself off; I picked up his cutlery and scattered it all over his kitchen floor. I flipped his table over (after some effort) and watched everything on top clatter onto the tiles. I found his books on one of his tables and threw them around the room. I opened his refrigerator and looked at a jug of water and thought about spitting in it, but didn't. I checked myself out in front of his small bathroom mirror: I looked at my red eyes and at how cute and tragic I looked whenever I cried. I fixed my makeup, fixed my hair. I lay on the couch.

It was strange, lying on that couch. I think it was the first time I was actually on it without Jacob happily by my side. It was where we'd sit whenever we'd have a quiet night in and watch DVDs, it was where we had our first kiss. I was completely depressed and couldn't stop crying, but once in a while I'd think of normal day-to-day things, like, "I forgot to drink milk this morning," or, "Maybe I should buy the latest Vogue or maybe I should just Google it" and, "Oh shit, I forgot to comment on that photo Mike uploaded, he's going to be pissed!" Then sometimes this huge nothingness would enter my mind: it was as if my soul and all of its thoughts would completely leave my body and it'd just be a cute little shell of me left behind on Jacob's favourite leather couch, existing for no reason but to fill space…

"What are you doing?"

I opened my eyes to see Jacob. His hair was messy and his eye bags looked deep and heavy.

He looked around without any sort of expression. "You trashed my apartment again."

"I hate you," was all I managed to say. I could feel tears forming around my eyes again. I glanced at my watch – I got there at six in the morning; it was now six in the evening. "Where were you?"

Jacob put his gym bag down (he still used the same leather bag I gave him on his birthday) and, moving my legs out of the way, slumped down on the couch next to me. "I don't care if you hate me." He pulled his mobile phone out of his pocket and tapped on the screen. "Oh. You rang me like a thousand times."

"I did. Where were you?"

"I was out."

"Of course you were." It was then that I couldn't help it. The tears began pouring down, one by one. I dotted my eyes with my fingers. Jacob didn't notice.

"We broke up," he said as he began texting someone. "Don't you get it? We're no longer together. Stop all this shit about killing yourself. I've tried and tried again to be nice to you about this. I've got nothing else to say. Grow up and move on. You've had your say and now you've trashed my place. But I'll let this go. Just go away. We've broken up. It's been months."

I pushed him. "Says who?"

"You agreed to this."

"I love you."

"You don't love me," he said. His phone vibrated and he checked it again. He sighed and responded.

"I do. If I didn't love you, I'd be sleeping normally."

"That's not love," he paused, typed another text message, and continued: "that's heartbreak."

I couldn't believe him. "You fucker! I'm heartbroken because I love you. I cut myself because I love you." I stood up and glared at him – he ignored me and kept writing a precious little text message. I sat back down and screamed into his couch: "I FUCKING HATE YOU SO MUCH! YOU KNOW THE SACRIFICES I MADE FOR YOU? YOU KNOW HOW MANY GUYS WERE AFTER ME?"

He sighed and put his phone down. "Stop pulling this crying shit on me. You promised you'd stop pulling this crying suicide bullshit on me!"

"I can't help it!"

"Yes you fucking can."

"Why aren't you hurting?" I sobbed. "Why aren't you hurting?"

He looked at me in the eyes for the first time since arriving. He put his hand on my knee. "You need to move on. When you do, you'll find a guy much better than me. Call your friends. Go drinking. Lose some weight. G –"

"Wait a minute. Lose some weight? *Lose some weight*?"

"I didn't mean it that way."

"How else did you mean it?"

Jacob shrugged, trying to look innocent. "It's just an expression. What I'm trying to say is, like, get a hobby, like join a gym."

"Fuck you," I said. "Look at yourself."

"I'm not fat."

"Yes you are. I can see your double chin," I lied.

He felt his chin and laughed slightly. "You're such a lying shit."

"You used to love me," I said.

"I still do."

"Then what are we doing?"

"It's a different love now, don't you see?"

"There's only one type of love," I said. "Love doesn't change."

"You and I both know you're lying."

"What if I'm not? What if I'm not lying?"

He rolled his eyes. "You're obviously lying. Love is just a word, and we abuse it and mould it to how we want it to appear to ourselves to make us feel better about the stupid things we do."

"Says you."

"Says the world."

Jacob's phone vibrated and before he could pick it up I grabbed his arm. "Please don't answer it. I promise I'll leave here soon. I know this'll be the last time we meet. Please, just don't, not right now. Please don't write another text message."

Jacob glared at me with a look of pure irritation. He considered something before relaxing his arm and putting his phone down. "It's important. I have to check this."

"It's her, isn't it?"

"You don't need to know."

"I do."

"You don't."

"Is it her?"

Jacob looked at his lap. "Yeah."

"What's so important that you have to text her right now?" I bravely decided to ask. "What are you texting about?"

"It's nothing."

"What are you texting about?"

"I don't think she likes me anymore," he shrugged, trying to look like he wasn't bothered.

"Why won't she like you?"

He sighed. "I guess I'm being needy. But it hurts when the girl just isn't bothered enough to reply to you like she used to. I spent this whole afternoon at her house and she's just a, she's just a… bitch. Like, it's always me who texts her first. It's always me who wants to do anything first. It didn't used to be like this. She used to be so excited to see me."

"You know what? I know exactly how you feel."

Jacob glanced at me, then looked back at his phone. I could tell that he really wanted to pick it up but I wished with everything that he wouldn't. There was a silence. A long, painful silence. Followed by Jacob: "I shouldn't be confiding this kind of stuff with you."

"You want to be friends, right? Then you can tell me anything."

He snickered. I felt like crying again.

"I can barely sleep anymore," he said.

"Like I said, I know how you feel."

We both let out a sad laugh.

"Your hair's gotten long," I eventually said. "Why's that?"

"You like it?"

"No. It's ugly. I liked it when it was shorter."

"You never like anything."

"That's not true," I said. "I like you." I put my legs on his lap and he let me. It felt good.

"You never used to say that."

"Say what?"

"That you like me."

"I'm saying it now."

He looked at my feet. "You have strange looking feet, you know that?"

"Shut up."

"Let me see your thighs," he said.

I lifted my skirt up a little and showed him.

He grimaced. "You've got to stop hurting yourself like that. It's not healthy."

"I don't know." I pulled my skirt back down. "I just feel like I need to feel the pain."

"But it's selfish."

"Tell me one person in this world who's not selfish."

"It's selfish," he said. "Other people care about you. Your mum. Your dad. Vail."

"Have you ever had a cry fantasy?"

"What's a cry fantasy?"

"Well, a cry fantasy is, it's like a secret fantasy you have where you imagine how your friends and loved ones would cry for you when you die. You think about how hurt they'd be and it'll make you sad, and you'll possibly even cry thinking about it, but like, it'll also make you secretly happy in a way, if you know what I mean? And then you'll imagine your funeral, and then you'll imagine who'll be there…"

Jacob said nothing. His eyebrows were creased.

"It's your care that I want, not anyone else's, don't you see that?" I said aloud. "I don't care about how anyone else feels. When I used to have a cry fantasy, I knew for sure you'd be there at my funeral, looking handsome in your suit and crying for me in front of all these people. But now, it hurts me to think that you won't be there at all."

"Are you living in some kind of movie? Don't you realise that there's more to life than a boy and a girl going on a few dates? You're sixteen. I'm eighteen. We've got the world ahead of us."

"The world started with a boy and a girl, Jacob."

"No it didn't. It started with a bang, followed by sea creatures and monkeys."

"Whatever. Whatever whatever whatever!" I looked at Jacob, at his tiredness and brokenheartedness. I wanted to kiss him all over and stab him all over. I missed him and didn't ever want to let him go. "You can save the world or whatever, but you can still also be in love with someone at the same time. You're pissing me off. There's nothing wrong with being in love with someone at the same time!"

"The whole game. The whole chasing. The whole pretending to not be interested in the people we're after, just so that they'd be interested in us for not being interested in them. It's fucked up. I hate relationships. I don't get why we need them when there are so many more important things to worry about in this world."

"Remember when you asked me out?" I suddenly remembered, giggling out of nowhere. "You were so scared."

"What? Oh yeah." Jacob smiled. "It was a challenge. And your dad. Geez."

"You're lucky my aunt wasn't there," I said, touching his cheek. "You were so cute. I don't want to leave you again."

"You will," he said. "Trust me, you will. The instant I place any sort of interest in you again."

"I won't."

"This is just a phase," he said. "Time will pass and you'll be embarrassed to admit about these past few months and you'd wish you didn't cut yourself and leave all those scars all over your body." He looked away. "And you'll meet someone much better than me."

"Fuck you. Like you're so wise. You're only two years older than I am."

"It's true though," he said.

"I just hate how this all is." I hugged him and cried and told him that I wanted to die, and eventually, he cried too and told me to stop hurting myself. He told me that he wanted to kiss me right now for all the wrong reasons and, with a strange tone of voice, he said that he couldn't handle all of my texts and cuts and begged me to let him move on. *So someone else can break your heart?* I asked. *I don't want anyone else to love you.* We sort of kissed and for an hour or so, I lay on his lap and he hesitantly held my hand. His hand was smooth and rough at the same time and it reminded me of no one.

"Somewhere in this world is someone like me."

"Somewhere in this world is someone who isn't."

"I want to walk on the sun."

"You'll burn. We'll be much better on the moon."

"You can't breathe on the moon."

"You definitely can't breathe on the sun."

"What was your favourite colour again?"

"Blue."

"I knew that."

"Sure you did."

"What happened to your nail?"

"I don't know. Wow, I just noticed that. What *is* that?"

"You're always daydreaming. You never notice *anything.*"

"I notice things."

"Like what? Remember when we got lost for hours?"

"We always got lost for hours."

"We should have a road trip."

"We've had a road trip before."

"I mean, like, a proper road trip, baby. Where we drive for days and days and days."

"Where would you want to go?"

"Anywhere."

"I'd rather go overseas."

"We never ended up going overseas. We always just spoke about it."

"We never ended up doing a lot of things. We mainly just had sex."

"Whatever. We did more than that."

"Like what?"

"I haven't even been to New Zealand."

"I know, but I want to go to Egypt first."

"Really? Egypt?"

"What's wrong with Egypt?"

"All the terrorists, honey."

"I told you so many times that I wanted to go to Egypt before and that I don't care about the terrorists. You don't even remember."

It was a perfect moment, and as the sun rose and as Jacob gradually fell asleep I walked to the bathroom and fixed my hair in front of the mirror. I stared at my face for some time. I loved my eyelashes. I walked back to Jacob and looked at him, innocent and asleep. *I'm going to text you when I go home or you will text me; it doesn't matter who will text first. What matters is that I'll tell you that I want us to be together again, and you'll agree. What matters is that I'm not going to leave you, and things will be normal again, just like on our first date, much before there was yelling and screaming and fighting and accusing, when you were so charming and you were clean shaven and you actually wore perfume and you kept asking me what I wanted to do and if I liked what I was eating; you kept*

 I picked his phone up and deleted all of the text messages from his girlfriend and deleted her phone contact. I changed his background photo to a photo of me. I put the phone back down. I watched him for some time before kissing his creased forehead. I walked to the balcony, untied our blanket and tenderly placed it over his body. I picked up a knife from the kitchen floor and lightly pushed its tip against his chest, right where his heart probably was. I watched his chest move up, and down, and up, and down. I thought about what would happen to me if I just killed him, if I hid his body somewhere or just left it there to rot. I wondered what would happen to me if I tortured him like how they torture people in the movies. If I just cut his lips off, then his eyelids, then his ears, and if he screamed I'd stab his stomach repeatedly while begging him to never forget me.

But then I realised I could never kill another person, especially him. I needed him in my life and he definitely needed me. I put the knife back down, right next to him so he'd know that I considered killing him but didn't do anything about it. I kissed his forehead one more time before leaving his keys on the carpet.

I walked to the car park and stepped inside my car and just sat there for a million hours, thinking about all these important and unimportant things again and again, just like I did on Jacob's couch. I thought about the time when I watched a movie in the cinema on my own for the first time and texted all of my friends about how much of a loser I was, or this time when I watched Jacob shave and he told me to stop staring because it made him feel awkward, or this time when a friend and I had a fight and I didn't know who to call so I spoke to my mum instead, and how she gave me the worst advice in the world. For a minute, my soul left me again, leaving a body in the car holding the steering wheel. My soul went up and down and left and right and saw things and remembered things and forgot about things, and when it became tired and started complaining about how much work it was to travel around the world it returned to my body, and I thought about the future really quickly, and I put my key in the ignition and drove home.

What Happened To Valentine's Day

We first decided that we knew what love is when were both around eight years old and we were on our bikes and you yelled, "Do you love me?" and I said, "Fuck yes!" and you giggled and you said, "Don't say the eff word, I hate it when you say the eff word," and I said, "But I love you – you have to accept me for everything that I am," and you smiled and said OK and we kept riding, and when we got home I proposed to you and you said yes, and we got married in front of your cat.

We both decided that we knew what love is when we were teenagers and we watched Jerry Maguire at home when nobody was around and there was a scene where Tom Cruise was humping a woman against a bookshelf. "Should we try this?" you asked and I said, "You had me at hello," and you held my hand and told me that you wanted a cute little kid like the kid in the movie and I said, "You can have anything you want," and deep inside I secretly hoped that our kid would be nothing like me.

We both found out what love is when you found someone else. You told me that he's cute and that he has a car and doesn't get angry like I do and that now you know what a real boyfriend is like. You no longer called me back or told me that you missed me like you used to and I couldn't sleep and I bought you flowers and told you, "I love you! I love you!" and you screamed, "Now you tell me! Now you tell me! After all these years you never told me, you never bought me flowers, not once!" and I threatened to punch the shit out of you and you said, "Go on, hit me, go on, hit me, go on, I hate you! Hit me!" and I didn't remind you about the time when we were eight years old.

We both found out what love is when we became responsible for money: we had to focus on our university studies and we then had to focus on our jobs and we then had to focus on our bills. I confessed to my girlfriend that I'd cheated on her, and her shoulders relaxed and she confessed that she'd cheated on me too, but even so we still hooked up once in a while when we were lonely or drunk or felt insecure; this kept happening until she thought that she was pregnant and didn't know who the father was and she became a lesbian and I sort of didn't hear from her again. That didn't matter, because by then all my friends and I wanted to do was to find hot girls to get into threesomes with. Sometimes I'd call you and tell you about my day and about the girls in my life and sometimes you'd call me and tell me your day and about the boys in your life and from how you'd describe your sex life with them I'd think: I'm so glad I never ended up with you.

We both found out what love is when we realised that love wasn't just about romantic love. I focused on getting promoted and learning the guitar on the internet and you focused on travelling all over the world and meeting interesting new people and learning new languages. One day I saw a video on the news of a woman being stoned to death and something about it struck me and I donated all of my savings, for some reason, to a cancer fund. Then there was a death and I was fired from my job. I began drinking with what little money I had left and spent weeks reading books in my room. You called and told me that you were engaged, and I got out of my rut and began applying for jobs overseas.

We both found out what love is when you started a family and I walked up to a girl in a cocktail party and asked her how she knew Leah. The girl and I talked for about ten minutes and I got her business card and the next day, after watching some porn (twice), I emailed her and we kept emailing until we finally met up for dinner and at the end of the night she smiled coyly and asked, "Is this a date?" and we kissed exactly like how we kissed the countless other dates we'd had in the past. I knew everything by then: what CDs to play in the background, how to unclasp a bra from behind or from the front, how to casually ask the girl if she was STD-free and had proof of a recent blood test, what kind of smell she'd have, what kind of goofy things you can do in bed to make her giggle, how she'd look the morning after, how I would look the morning after. One evening you called me and told me how much you loved your son and your husband and, tears in my eyes, I told you that I was happy for the both of us: you were married to a wonderful man and I was married to a template.

We both found out what love is when I bumped into you somewhere very Hollywood and very cliché: a café bookshop. You'd certainly aged and gained some weight but you made me laugh and I missed you nonetheless. You told me endless stories about your husband and your son and your dog and I didn't know what to say, so I talked about my career, some people at work, about how I go to the gym three times a week. You put your hand on mine and said, "You'll find her, you will," and, looking straight at you, I told you, "Are you fucking blind?" and you giggled and said, "Don't say the eff word, I hate it when you say the eff word," and I asked you if you still liked to ride bikes in parks.

Eva, Part Four: Dancing

I leant forward and grinned at Eva. "Is there any shit on my teeth?"

She looked closely at my teeth before pinching my nose. "No, baby, you're completely fine."

I was in a suit I borrowed from a friend and she was wearing this green thing that made her look prettier than she already was. We were at a formal gathering full of awful music and awful people. I stood up and offered her my hand. "Let's, like, dance or something."

She stood up. "Okay, smooth talker. Take my breath away."

I took her hand and we went to the dance floor. I put my arm around her waist and sort of moved my feet around. "I'm a terrible dancer, Eva," I said. "This is all I can do."

"For once in our relationship, I think you're actually right."

I pinched her arse. "What perfume are you wearing?"

"It's just soap," she said. "As tacky as you might think it is, the new Kylie perfume is pretty good. Francesca's boyfriend bought her a bottle and it smells so good. You should buy it for me."

"Done and done," I lied. I had no money whatsoever.

"Have you heard from the competition yet?"

"I lost," I sighed, hoping that she'd somehow never ask me about it. Earlier that year I joined The Australian/Vogel's Literary Award, a literary competition where winning entries were awarded twenty thousand dollars. I was so confident in my writing that I bragged to everyone that I'd win the twenty thousand dollar prize through my thirty-five thousand word story submission, and so did Eva, who also bragged to everyone she knew that I would win the prize. "It turns out that my story wasn't good enough."

Eva said nothing for a while. I looked at her expression closely and knew what she was thinking. "Well, how about the other competition you joined? The one about the guy who fed his girlfriend so much food she exploded was really good. Remember how it made me cry and how you laughed at me? Did you win that one?"

I also joined a Brisbane State Library short story competition where winners were awarded with twenty five hundred dollars. "No," I mumbled. "I got a rejection letter last week."

"Oh." She bit her lip. "Well, don't worry about it. There are plenty more competitions out there."

"When I finally get that publishing contract, we'll finally be able to travel all over the world. That crime author I met at the writer's festival. He got a seven hundred thousand dollar advance. Imagine that. Seven hundred kay." The song changed. "Shall we continue dancing?"

"I don't mind."

I spun her around and she giggled. "I missed you," I

said.

"I missed you too."

"It's been a while," I said.

"I'm sorry, honey. I've just had so many assignments."

"You went out the other night," I reminded her.

"Yeah well that was just for Francesca's birthday party. Cut me some slack. You're always out, even if you keep saying you have no money to take me out for dinner."

"I really don't have money. And I'm busy, too. Writing a novel isn't as easy as it sounds. Plus I've got some really good short story ideas. Like this one story about this guy who kidnaps this kid and –"

"Why don't you get a job?"

"Are you serious?" I stopped moving. "I can't believe you just said that."

Eva shrugged. "What's wrong with what I said? You can't just continue living from savings and the government, Dean."

"You just want presents like your friends do."

Eva was about to yell something at me but thankfully Jacob arrived, patting us both on the back. He was red in the face and his eyes were bloodshot and his breath smelt like cigarettes and whiskey. "You know a couple is in love when they even touch each other's teeth," he grinned. "That's right, you fucking love birds." He looked at Eva. "You were putting your hands right in Dean's mouth earlier. I saw you!"

Eva sort of smiled.

"We're fighting," I told Jacob. "Okay to piss off for a while?"

Jacob laughed and stumbled off.

"Why are you crying?" I frowned at Eva and tried to run my thumb under her eye, but she pulled away from me and wiped her tears away herself.

"Just so much on my mind."

We finished the song, silently, and walked outside. I held Eva's hand.

"I want to smoke," she said.

"You said you'd quit smoking if I do."

"Well," she let go of my hand, "I need a smoke."

I pulled a carton out of my jacket pocket and handed it to her. She looked surprised. "Why do you have cigarettes in your pocket?"

"I couldn't do it. I failed."

For some reason, we both laughed at this. It wasn't even funny. Eva had a strange laugh: her shoulders would move up and down as she snorted a little.

"I hate your laugh!" this made us both laugh even more. "Let's go home."

"You don't want to say goodbye to Jacob?"

"He's high," was all I said.

Eva giggled and, wrapping both of her arms around one of mine, leant her head against my shoulder and told me that she loved me.

The Things We Do For
Those Who Don't Love Us

I knew that I was in love with this particular wolf because I'd gone out with three other wolves beforehand, and they were nowhere near as good.

Besides the fact that all of my friends believed that he was totally cute and that he listened to indie music like I did, I suppose I also loved him because he was tall and texted me a lot and made ten million dollars a year, most of it from his parents.

But I guess, like, the only problem about him was me. He just didn't seem to love me as much as I wanted him to.

"I already love you," he reassured me tenderly. "You know that. But for me to love you as much as you want me to, you have to do three things."

"What are those three things, baby?"

"Before I begin telling you about these three things, I have to warn you: each of my requests will get more and more painful for you," he said, his paws gently resting on my shoulders. "And I have a gut feeling that once you complete one of my requests, you won't be able to stop trying to get the rest of them, no matter how painful they may be. On top of this, there's also no guarantee that I'll love you any more so afterwards. Are you sure you want to do this?"

I was hesitating inside, but I didn't want to show it. "Of course I can, baby. I'll do anything for you to love me."

"Fine. Firstly," he started, "I want you to colour your hair blonde. Don't get me wrong, I like brunettes and all, but blondes turn me on so much more. I had a crush on a blonde girl when I was a kid, and I think if you turn yourself blonde, I'll fall in love with you like I did with her." He put three thousand dollars in my hand and sent me away to find the flashiest hairdresser in the city.

The process took like, fifty hours, but afterwards, it was totally worth it. I looked hot. Even my best friend Vail, who came with me, complimented me, and she rarely complimented me. I texted a photo of me with my new hairstyle to all of my friends and they called me gorgeous, and this sounds a little cheeky, but I agreed.

I knew it: my wolf had a great taste in women. I hurried home to show him my new do, but he wasn't there. Instead, he left a note on my pillow:

Sorry darling, working late. You're now blonde! That's electrifying. Sure, it's not a natural blonde and you can't get natural blue eyes to match, but I guess it'll do. Here's the second thing you have to do: I want you to never remove your makeup. I love Barbie dolls because no matter how much you wash them, their makeup remains the same. You human women love fooling people with your makeup so much you might as well have it on all the time – if you are any other way, all this shows is that you're ashamed of how you really look. I've emailed you a first class ticket for you to go to the US and see the best surgeons, personal trainers and cosmetic tattooists in the world who'll fix the ugly shape of your nose, burn off all the excess fat on you I never liked and finally, tattoo the makeup on you just the way I want it. This will be very painful. If you still want to do this, I've transferred four million dollars into your account for your accommodation and expenses. Love you.

He was right: it *was* a very painful and lengthy journey. But he was really sweet and thoughtful about it all because he'd text me with a, *How'd it go?* after each operation and work out session. Also, not only did I become much better looking, I was also able to travel all around the US and see landmarks like Times Square and the Grand Canyon. I did so much shopping! Besides all the pain and stress involved with my makeover, it was easily the best holiday I'd been on in my entire life.

But don't get me wrong or anything – even though the US was a lot of fun, all I could think about was flying back home to my wolf and just lying in bed with him and smelling his fur.

After a few long months, I finally returned home. I immediately ran up to our bedroom, but he wasn't there. The room looked unusually clean. On top of our wardrobe was a long-winded note:

I'm sorry I couldn't pick you up from the airport, honey – I'm out with my friend Kath. She's fantastic company, you should meet her. Anyway, I saw your photos: you look beautiful. Very beautiful. But I guess genetically you're a little more big boned than others and, judging from the photos I've seen of you online, you still don't look that great on some angles (especially when flash is involved). But at least you almost tried your best. Anyway, looks aren't everything without personality and character to back them up. There's something about your personality that irritates me sometimes. You sound uneducated. You're not attractively independent. You're not challenging. You don't listen to me enough and respond with engaging dialogue during times when I want you to. You only know one language. You're not seductively wild yet obedient and loyal. You don't give me blowjobs when I want and you don't even swallow! What's wrong with you? If you still want to continue with my last request, I want you to give me back all the money I've given you that you haven't spent yet. I want you to start with nothing to humble your proud and stupid self, and I want you to find a way to fly back to the US and get into college with the little that you currently know and study law in Yale while working part time; while this is happening, you must also study French, Mandarin and visual art during the spare hours you have. Every second Wednesday evening, you shall recite poetry at my friend Jean Pedro Kanato Migemono Dante Suresh the Third's Jazz Club in New York and form lasting friendships with the eccentrics in that club. You must exercise at least three hours a week and only eat purely organic food that clears the skin, tones muscles, prevents cancer, boosts your immune system and tastes like absolute shit. On your second year, you must work somewhere famous, you must obtain an internship in an advertising agency such as Ogilvy, a magazine such as Vogue or a publication such as the New York Times. On our bed, I've also placed the complete works of Oscar Wilde, which you must memorise by the time we meet again. You must never, not once, swerve from these goals because it will mean me losing interest in you: do not panic – this experience will add to your already outstanding (yet kind of forced) physical beauty and will make many men and many of the world's most desirable wolves, including myself, fall madly in love with you. Do this, and I shall love you until the day I die.

I put the note down and cried for probably like, four hours. Doing something like that was something I thought I'd never do, it was something I'd never been raised to do. But I trusted my wolf and I loved him more than anything and he'd been right about what he'd told me so far: I did have a funny nose and I did have excess fat and I did look better blonde and I did look better with permanent makeup. He always challenged me, and I always ended up better because of it.

I never had to endure so many sleepless nights in my life, but I did it: I was accepted into Yale, I graduated from Law, I became fluent in both French and Mandarin, I obtained an internship at Vogue and was even promoted. I read all of Oscar Wilde's works and took particular interest in an essay of his about socialism. I mingled with famous poets; I wrote poetry and even published poetry. Slowly, but surely, I gained a stronger understanding of the world by reading about it; I developed standards I once never had; I became familiar with art and relationships and the dynamics of the world economy; I became educated and attractive people took me more seriously, especially since I usually walked around with a copy of the *New York Times*; I lost my old friends and gained new and more successful ones; I worked past midnight, I cried past midnight, I grew past midnight, and at the end of my twenty-seven-hour days I'd smile and fantasise about my wolf, my wolf who lovingly made me who I've become – I now looked at the mirror every morning more carefully and disappointedly than ever, and from what I'd see I'd plan how I could improve myself so that my wolf would love me more than anything.

I flew home with a first class ticket I purchased on my own. I hadn't seen my wolf in over seven years but I thought about him for what felt like a thousand. I looked at our mansion: it still looked beautiful. How I missed it! My heart beating quickly, I opened the door and ran inside. There, smiling with pride, underneath our expensive and regularly maintained chandelier light, was my wolf, waiting for me in all of his handsome glory. We ran to each other: my wolf greeted me by biting me, and I bit him back, and we spun around the room and tackled each other and fell inside a dark shadow of love.

You'll totally love this next part because it was just so cute and so natural: he told me to close my eyes, and when I opened them, right in front of me was a ring, a three million dollar diamond ring. "You are now, in your own right, a very desirable woman. Sure, you're a little older and saggier now than when I first met you and I've noticed five more wrinkles along your forehead, but I'm sure you can slow that ugliness down if you just put in a bit of effort every night and morning and actually try for once. But we'll talk about that later. As promised, I love you more than ever and would like nothing more than to spend the rest of my life with you."

It felt so perfect and so right. Tears pouring out of my eyes, I nodded immediately and said, "I do! I love you I love you I do! I love you so much. I want to be by your side forever and ever and ever. I love you so much and have waited for this moment for so long!"

We divorced after about three months. He told me that he'd accidentally fallen in love with his friend Kath, who wasn't blonde, who didn't jog for half an hour at five in the morning every morning, who didn't know anything about Oscar Wilde. He looked at me with a sad look and said, "You try too hard. You're just not the same girl I fell in love with, and it hurts to see you this way."

I cried for days, weeks, months, years. I kept thinking back on everything that I could've done wrong and spent hours with my girlfriends just talking about my wolf, about why he'd leave me, and we'd always end our conversations with the same conclusion: I just wasn't good enough. Although I spent hundreds of thousands of dollars further improving my appearance, he never returned my calls or opened his door to me. If only he knew that I never stopped loving him. If only he knew that everything I did, I did for his acceptance.

In the end I married a pigeon I didn't love, but he loved me more than anything and my best friends said that's what's important. He even implanted eagle wings into his back just to impress me. I died before he did, which was perfectly fine with me.

In The Name Of Love

Ribbon always dreams about flying. I saw this video once, this short video of this boy, his arms outstretched, flying. He had this stupid smile on his face and he was flying. I don't know where he was flying to or from or if it was his first time to fly. I don't even remember where I saw the video or how long the video went for or who I was with. It doesn't matter. All I remember is his blue shirt and his shorts and his bare feet and his stupid bloody smile. I've never dreamt of flying and I don't think I ever will.

"I'm horny."

I looked at Ribbon up and down. "You're always fucking horny." I scratched my arm. "Stop always being so fucking horny."

Ribbon and I didn't do much. Ribbon was pretty useless and so was I. Ribbon was pregnant and she went around punching these bastard boys and I always went around helping her because it felt great. Do it and don't doubt me. Go to someone and punch them on their ugly face and don't you tell me it doesn't feel great.

Ribbon didn't say anything so I kept going. "If you weren't so horny in the first place then you wouldn't be as fat as you are now."

She crossed her head. "You never feel horny?"

"Why would I want to feel horny for?" I looked at a guy passing us. "You think I'd ever want one of those ugly small logs in me?"

Ribbon cackled. "Why not? You should see the look on their faces when you do it." Ribbon thought about something before smiling like I'd never seen her smile before. "You just shove them in your cunt and they'll do anything you want."

"It's fucking shit." I jabbed Ribbon's stomach. "All it will do is make me fat and ugly like you."

"I'm pregnant, cunt."

"You're fucking fat."

Ribbon punched my arm. "I'm pregnant."

"I don't care, bitch. You're fat and you just got pregnant so you can win more fights." Ribbon was thirty-five years old and I was sixteen. It'd been a month since we'd been in a fight, and we only won the last one because no one wanted to bash a pregnant lady.

We were in the city and it was a bit past midnight and it was boring. Jeff the copper was near us and he was pretending to talk into his radio. Jeff was about Ribbon's age and we always gave him shit. *Jeff, I'll fucking kill you!* we'd yell to him sometimes, and he'd give us the finger, laughing, and his partner, who always seemed to be different, would always look worried. We first met him when Harold started beating Ribbon across the head. Jeff came and took him away and gave Ribbon some money afterwards.

Jeff! You look like a faggot in that uniform!

Jeff! Your dad wants you to suck his dick!

Everyone hates coppers and I guess I would too if it

wasn't for cunts like Jeff. Jeff's pretty ugly, but he gives us money, and he helps Ribbon once in a while. He always smiles at all the shit we tell him and asks us how we are, even if we keep calling him a faggot. He keeps telling me to go back to school, like he's the smartest fucking guy. If you were a smart guy you wouldn't be a copper. If you were a smart guy you'd kill yourself.

We were bored that night, so we tried to catch Jeff's attention.

"Jeff!" Ribbon yelled. "Come here!"

Jeff glanced at us, but then kept talking to his partner.

"Fuckin' pig!" Ribbon yelled. "Come here!"

Eventually, Jeff walked over to us. He smiled. "Good evening. What's pissing you off tonight, ladies?"

Ribbon nudged me. "Fucking Eksie here thinks I'm fat."

Jeff looked at Ribbon, then at me. "She's pregnant."

"She's fat."

Jeff laughed.

"What's so funny, cunt?" I stood up, looking at them both. "It's fucking disgusting." I pointed at Ribbon. "She's disgusting." I pointed at Jeff. "You're disgusting." I pointed at Ribbon again. "You're gonna shit that little thing out and it's gonna look all retarded like Jeff. Down syndrome and all that shit."

Ribbon just kept on laughing, even if it wasn't a joke.

Jeff glanced at his partner and a bunch of other coppers standing by the mall and mouthed something that sounded like, "It's okay." He looked at us. "Not much yelling tonight, alright? And don't start any fights."

"You're a faggot, Jeff. You're fucking shit."

Jeff looked at his watch. "You should be going home now. Both of you."

"This is boring."

"Let's go somewhere."

"Jeff's a fucking cunt."

Ribbon and I ignored whatever else Jeff was saying to us and started randomly walking anywhere like we usually did back then. We just walked and walked, as far as possible from the lights and the laughing couples and the people leaving pubs and the ugly coppers.

We stopped walking when we eventually spotted a guy we wanted to roll. Ribbon nudged me and pointed at him. I think I smiled but I don't really remember. We followed him. He was with his wife or his girlfriend or sister or partner or whatever. He was wearing a black shirt and jeans and even though I hadn't seen his face yet, I knew that he'd be ugly. They were always ugly. These men, these ugly faggots, they know that you're following them but they pretend like they don't know that you're following them. If they glance back at you, they only glance back at you quickly, because they're scared. They always want to act like they're kings, even if they're scared. But don't worry, kings act tough but they'll always cry. You'll always find a way to make them cry.

"Oi, cunt!" Ribbon yelled out. They ignored her so she yelled again and again until they stopped and turned around. The ugly man looked frightened, which was good. His partner or whatever grabbed his arm.

"Where's our wallet?" I asked the ugly faggot.

"What?"

"Where's our wallet, cunt?"

His partner or whatever was crying. She was constantly whispering something to him as he kept whispering back, asking her to be quiet.

Ribbon and I stood there, not saying anything to him, until he finally took his wallet out and handed it to us.

Ribbon looked into his wallet. "I'm pregnant, and this is all you give us?"

The ugly man didn't say anything.

"Fuckin' ugly cunt." I spat on the ground and we walked away from them, back towards the lights of the city. For a while, I didn't think of much. I just focused on our footsteps. Ribbon always walked slower than me, even before she became fat. She'd always be the one breathing hard, yelling for me to slow down. She was such an old, fat bitch.

We ended up at this bottle shop. Ribbon told me to wait outside for a while. I stood around, sometimes spitting, whatever. I looked at the girls passing by. I just stood there and looked at all of them. You put them all in a room and they're all the same, they're all trying to make some cunt happy. I wasn't trying to make some cunt happy. Too many people are trying to make some cunt happy, even if nobody actually ends up happy. If they didn't have to smile to be polite, everyone would just wrinkle and scowl and complain and secretly want to be ugly. What's wrong with being ugly? Why is ugly even a word?

Ribbon came back out with a carton. I looked at the bottle shop for a second and then followed her back towards the dark. We kept walking until we got to some building near my old house. We looked for the darkest area we could find. We sat down and took turns drinking from the carton.

"I'm horny!" Ribbon screamed.

"I'll kill your ugly baby if you say that again!"

Ribbon stood up, but then sat back down. She drank some more. She was dribbling a bit but I didn't tell her. "Do you really think my baby will be ugly?"

"Of course, you bitch. As ugly as your dirty fucking cunt lips." She didn't say anything. I looked at Ribbon's stomach. "You've been bashed so many times and you're still smoking and getting drunk," I said. "You dumb faggot. You've gotta stop it if you don't want your kid to look like Jeff."

"What's wrong with Jeff? I reckon he looks alright."

I couldn't believe her. "The fucking copper Jeff?"

"Who else?"

I slapped her knee. "You're fucked in the head, you know that? You don't want your kid looking like some cunt copper."

"You told me you were one of the smartest girls in school."

"Like shit I did."

"You were," she insisted. "Your uniform had badges and shit on it. Don't fucking lie to me!"

"School is full of ugly sluts and ugly teacher cunts who don't care about anything else except how much they're getting paid. Let's burn it." I suddenly had a good idea. "Let's buy one of those petrol jugs or whatever from the station, they're cheap as, and spread the shit all over my school and fuckin' burn it."

"It's your school, Eksie. You can't burn your own

school."

"Fuck you, you old bitch. I'm doing it with or without you."

"Fine," Ribbon said. "We're doing it tomorrow night then." She thought for a moment. "But I'm stopping you halfway."

We kept drinking until it all ran out. Ribbon fell asleep. For once, she didn't vomit. I remember watching her for a long time. I stroked some of her hair. I watched her breathe. Sometimes she'd chew on something that didn't exist. Her lips were pale. She never made me pay her for anything, never complained about me. She was the only person in the world who was decent. I looked at her lips again. I kissed them, moved back, and looked at them. They didn't change; they were always the same, always looking like that. Ribbon was breathing like nothing mattered at all. Ribbon was always right.

I wiped my eyes. I stood up and walked and walked and walked and ended up at my house. It was big and it was the only house in the neighbourhood that wasn't all lit up by lights or whatever. I felt dizzy. I found a few rocks and pelted them at the front door, at the windows.

"Fuck you, cunt!"

I threw more.

"Fuck you!"

I ran up to the front door and beat it with my palms. I kept yelling. I beat it with my fists until it hurt too much. The door opened and I saw Mum's face through the screen door. I hadn't seen her in a year. Her hair was messy like mine. "Elena?"

"Fuck you!"

"Elena?" Mum opened the screen door. "Elena?"

I pointed at her. I don't remember what I said.

I heard an ugly man's voice. Mum turned around and said something like, "She's drunk."

My dad stepped out of the house. "It's four in the fuck–"

I swung at him and knocked him right across his head. I was a big girl and he was a small, dirty man. He was still standing so I charged him and knocked the ugly faggot to the ground and punched him again and again. My mum was screaming. My dad landed a few punches but I didn't care. My mum ran out of the door and knelt against my dad. She was screaming and crying for help. She didn't look up at me. I wanted to kick her but didn't. I don't remember everything that I said. In the end I just pointed at her, shaking, but she never looked up at me. With all the billions of people in the world, only the three of us could have ever fully understood it all.

I walked back to Ribbon. I remember it being early morning by then. She was sleeping, slumped up against a wall. I sat down next to her. I was bleeding somewhere. I thought about this time, when I was little, when my mum and dad bought our first house. I wanted the room with the biggest window. I pictured my bed in there, what I'd see first when I'd wake up. I pictured the posters I'd have. I pictured where I'd put my table and my school books and school bag. I pictured where I'd hang my clothes. I wanted the same pink picture frames that my best friend had. I gave mum a list of everything I wanted her to buy to make my room the best out of everyone else's. I told a lot of people a lot of things. I did a lot of things. I dreamt of a lot of things. I put Ribbon's hand in mine and just sat there, leaning against the wall like she was, waiting for her to wake up.

Eva, Part Five:
The Terrible Things We Do

Eva told me the bad news when we were in the back seat of my car, sweating, bottomless, and I asked her, "You love me, right?" and at first one tear came out of her, then another tear, and then more tears and I knew what was coming. Her friend who was visiting from Sydney, the one who she used to work with at the photo shop when she was fourteen, returned to Brisbane for a holiday and wanted to take her out for dinner. He took her to some expensive seafood restaurant in South Bank and paid for the meal and afterwards they drove to a parking spot near the river, to talk and catch up. They kissed for a while, and he wanted to take her to the back seat but she cried and refused, so he drove her home, complaining that he spent all this money to visit her and all they did was make out.

"He was being a wolf. A bloody wolf."

I leant back and we stared at each other in silence. A moment passed before I decided to put my shorts back on. "Why did you do this?"

"He has money, he's stable, and I know this sounds bad, but, but he's better looking than you," she said, now crying louder. "Break up with me I'm so sorry please break up with me. It's you I love, I'm so sorry, please break up with me."

"You cheating bitch!" I yelled a bunch of other things before calming myself down. I looked outside my windscreen: all I could see was a wall. It was about one in the morning and we were parked in a shopping centre's outdoor car park. "Before we end things for good I have something to tell you."

"What?"

"I hooked up with Madison," I said.

There was a silence. Eva slowly sat up. "What?"

"It was during that month when we kept breaking up and getting back together. You broke up with me and that night, I went to Madison's apartment and we hooked up. I didn't know when to tell you, so I guess this is the right time. I was so sick of you always breaking up then making up with me, and unlike you, she's actually a decent person inside."

There was more silence, until: "How far did you go?"

"Do you really want to know?" I asked her.

"Just tell me!"

"Halfway."

For a moment, Eva stared at me hard. Eyebrows tensed, her eyes moved up and down over my face, looking for any trace of dishonesty. Her eyebrows then relaxed and saddened – she let out a long, loud wail. I'd never seen someone cry that loudly in my life.

"And you weren't going to tell me?" She opened the door and ran out of my car.

"Wait!" I yelled out for her. "You're completely bottomless!"

"I don't give a fuck you went halfway, you hypocrite!"

I closed the door and got to the front seat of the car and drove slowly behind her, repeatedly beeping and high beaming her from behind. She walked unexpectedly fast; her arse was incredibly firm – for a moment I just watched both cheeks bounce up and down. I sped up to drive next to her, and as I did I thought about running her over.

I opened the passenger door. "Get in, Eva."

"Why did you do it, baby?" She kept walking.

"Why did *you* do it?"

"Bye, Dean."

I glanced around worriedly. "Listen, if you don't get in my car you're going to get raped. You're going to get raped by a bear and I won't be man enough to fight it off."

"This is no time to make your stupid jokes!"

"I'm not joking! Can you please just get in? Just get the hell in!"

"There aren't any bears here."

"Just get in!"

She got in the car and put her underwear and skirt back on. She held my hand as we drove home in silence.

Vail Before It Ended

I have a lot of memories of Vail, and although there were a lot of good memories and bad memories, there were also a lot of in-betweens. Most of these memories are now vague and unreliable, but there was one particular day I spent with Vail that I can't forget. Which is stupid, because there was nothing important about that day whatsoever. It was merely a day in our relationship; there weren't any natural disasters or celebrity deaths or tragedies with loved ones – it was just a day with Vail and me and the sun and the moon and cars and all that other shit, but I remember every single bit of it: everything we said, everything we did, what she wore, what I wore and what noises and smells were in the background. The memory, as stupid and boring as it may sound to you, just sits with me, no matter how much older I get and how much further Vail and I drift apart.

"So?"

"So what?"

"What?" I rubbed my eyes and opened them completely. "What time is it?"

Vail threw a pillow at me and giggled. "You've been sleep talking, you weirdo."

"Really? What did I say?"

She rolled over and put her arm over my chest. "A lot of it was incoherent. In the end you kept saying, 'So? So?' like a tough guy."

"I remember having a few dreams, but I don't remember what about."

"I remember *my* dream," she said, leaning her forehead against my shoulder. "Want to know what happened in my dream?"

"What happened in your dream?"

"I befriended this guy from Sportsgirl."

I played with her hair a little, hoping that her story would end soon so that we could eat breakfast. "*Sportsgirl?*" I smirked.

"Yeah, I know, right? This guy, like, he never spoke. But I fed him and took care of him and one day, he turned into a monster."

"You've got a fucked up mind, Miss Vail."

"Do you think dreams have meanings?"

I shrugged, looking around the room for a cigarette.

Vail pinched my cheek. "They're all out, honey."

"We smoked that much?"

"We've got to quit one day, Dean."

"Says who?"

"Says our health."

"What's the time?"

Vail fumbled around and found a mobile phone. "It's only nine in the morning." She stretched her arms out, closed her eyes and smiled in satisfaction. "Let's go back to bed. Let's sleep forever."

"But we have to check out at ten, remember?"

"Oh yeah. I can't believe we have to check out so

soon. It feels like there's so much more lazing around we have to do. And I'm hungry."

That was my cue. "Let's have breakfast. What do we have?"

She sat up. "I'll have a look."

We both stepped out of the bed. I headed for the couch while Vail walked to the kitchen of the studio we were staying in. It was a decent studio. It was modern and spacious and there was a large TV and DVD player; it had a large balcony and on some evenings we'd completely stop talking and just look outside and think of things that weren't related to the view at all.

Vail called out from the kitchen. "We've got like, four eggs. And cereal. Since you made breakfast yesterday, I'll make some scrambled eggs for you today."

"Thank you, ma'am." I sat down on the couch and stared at the TV. It wasn't on and all I could see was a vague reflection of myself. I looked sleepy and warped all over. I leant forward, rubbing my fingers against my forehead. "Is there any bread left?"

"There's one piece of toast."

"You have it," I said.

"I'm not hungry. You can have it."

"No seriously," I said. "You can have it."

"I'm not that hungry, Dean."

"You sure?"

"Yes, I'm sure, Dean. You're a boy. You should eat more than I do."

Vail ended up eating the toast and most of the scrambled eggs. The morning was one of those quiet, dewy mornings where everything outside looked like what I believed London would look like outside: wet, cool, kind of green and grey. We ate at the balcony in silence for a while until Vail, tapping her plate with her fork and looking at me, started talking again.

"I still have to decide whether dreams have meanings, like if they give us advice we should follow, or if they're merely just our random thoughts presented in strange ways."

"Can't they be a bit of both?" I asked her. "So if you dream of, let's say, having sex with the mailman, then your dream is trying to tell you that you wanted to have sex with a mailman, which is actually something you considered earlier in the day."

"But aren't dreams much more complicated than that? I remember like, this recurring nightmare I used to have when I was a kid. It was of a giant steel ball overlooking this tiny city. Me saying it now doesn't make it sound like a nightmare whatsoever, but experiencing that dream – experiencing that nightmare, it would like, cause me to wake up in cold sweats. That giant ball scared the shit out of me so much, but I'm absolutely sure I'd never thought of giant steel balls – don't be immature, Dean – while awake before. Which brings me to back to my question: what do nightmares and dreams mean? Are they like, messages from another world? Should I even try and interpret them?"

I suddenly wanted a beer. "I suppose we can interpret dreams all we want, but the only way we'll know the truth about anything in life is when we die."

"Unless when we die, that's it, we just die." Vail remembered something and gave me an angry sort of smile.

"And I have never thought of sleeping with a mailman."

"Why? What's wrong with mailmen?"

"You know what I mean."

I left Vail at the balcony and headed to our room. I scanned over all the mess we'd made over the past few days and picked up a half-filled bottle of red wine. I looked it over before coming back out to the balcony.

"There's still some wine."

"We can drink it tonight," Vail suggested. "At my place."

"We can drink it now," I said.

Vail frowned and checked her phone. "It's only nine thirty, Dean. We should pack up and check out soon."

I ignored her: I finished the water in my cup and poured some wine in it. I was about to pour some wine into her own cup but she pulled it away. "It's early, honey. Let's drink the rest tonight."

"It'll be off by then."

She smirked. "It's probably off right now."

"You drank the other morning and I didn't complain." I took a sip of the wine. Vail muttered "whatever" and began texting someone on her phone; no one spoke, so I continued drinking the wine until I finished the entire cup. Vail picked our plates up and walked towards the kitchen. I watched her walk for a moment: she was in short, lime-coloured cotton shorts (they were so short I could see her arse cheeks) and a black singlet that looked simple but was probably painfully expensive. Her hair was a little messy, but not that messy, and she walked like a woman who could dominate the bedroom, who could ruin any man she laid her eyes on.

She wasn't wearing a bra. I filled my cup with wine again and stared at the view outside the balcony and thought about how there were so many cars driving past us and about this lady I once had a thing with, and how she kept asking me to tweak her large nipples.

I walked inside and put some jeans on and changed my shirt to a plain black one. In the corner I saw Vail take her top and shorts off and hop into a summer dress – a tan, slightly transparent dress with faded flower prints all over it.

"Vail?"

"Yeah? I'm getting dressed."

I said nothing.

***

We brushed our teeth and packed our belongings and checked out of the studio. We walked to the parking lot and put our things in the boot of Vail's BMW before walking to the front and sitting inside.

"Where to now, mister?" Vail asked as she put her seatbelt on.

"We've been everywhere in Brisbane."

"You're right. And we've been everywhere in Queensland."

"I suppose that's it." I put my sunglasses on. "We've done everything we can. We might as well die."

"Shall I drive off a cliff?"

"Why not? That way, we can die together."

"You're so fantastically romantic, Dean."

"I try my best."

126

Vail drove fast, much faster than I did. She never seemed to care – probably because she'd always gotten away with it. She seemed to know when and where to speed or cross a red light and not get caught or get anyone killed; she'd never even received a speeding ticket. Ever.

We ended up parking in South Bank, beneath the Gallery of Modern Art. For those of you who don't know, South Bank is a parkland area situated near the Brisbane's Central Business District. In South Bank is its popular manmade beach, the Gallery of Modern Art, a few museums, restaurants, riverside walkways, one of the most affordable cinemas in Brisbane, a piazza of some sort and a towering white Ferris Wheel called the Wheel of Brisbane.

"You know what?" she said, looking up at the Gallery of Modern Art. "I don't think I've actually been here before."

"We have," I told her disappointedly. "We went here last year. With Jude and that."

"What? When?"

"After that guy's party. Your friend, What'shisname, the Asian."

"Which friend?"

I tried to remember Vail's friend, but all I could vaguely recall was what he looked like and the white t-shirt he wore. It said FUCK ME MAN I'M OLD ENOUGH. "He had like a beard, and we kept laughing at his mashed potato jokes. He was Japanese."

"Oh, Kenneth?"

"Yeah, Kenneth."

Vail laughed. "I remember now. You're right – we have been here. We all went to this fancy arts presentation in the evening and drank all the free champagne. You puked."

"I didn't puke," I said.

"Yes you did."

"Anyway let's talk about better things. Like your nice, smooth legs."

I started pinching her legs and she ran away, giggling. "You're an idiot, honey."

"Let's not go in the gallery yet," I said. "Let's go for a walk."

"Sure."

We held hands and headed out of the parking lot and out towards the lawns facing the Brisbane River. There weren't that many people around and it seemed as though the dewiness outside our studio apartment followed us all the way to where we were: the sun was hidden behind bits and pieces of grey and everything felt slightly cool and damp. The air smelt crisp; in the distance you could hear a car or two, but they were far away. Everything felt calm. Being outside was a good change from lazing around inside the cramped apartment, drinking and eating and smoking for three whole days.

I raised Vail's hand and spun her around. She giggled and embraced me.

"We should travel," she suggested, snuggling into my arms.

"Where would you want to go?"

"Egypt. Or Tokyo. Or New York."

"Let's go somewhere strange," I said.

"What? Like Iran or something?" She laughed.

"Why not? It'll be great."

"I'll get stoned to death."

"Not every woman in Iran gets stoned to death. Just some of them."

"I want to go to Tokyo," Vail said, ignoring me. "Then ski in the islands up north. A friend of mine – you know Michelle? White Michelle, not the Latina one. She just came back from skiing there. It just looks so, like, beautiful in Japan. It's four seasons, too, and every season looks amazing."

"I thought you've already been to Japan." We sat down on some grass and I leant backwards, looking at the river in front of us.

"I did but I was young. I was supposed to go on exchange in high school but I was too hung up over a stupid ex-boyfriend of mine. He was like, really jealous and didn't want me to go anywhere without him."

"You've told me that story already."

"Oh yeah."

"And I've already been to Japan, remember?"

"But only during winter. How about New York? I'm sure you'll have plenty of things to write about if you went to New York. I miss shopping there. Fashion here is just so backwards."

"I'd love to go to New York. But I'll need some money first. A ticket itself will already cost me a lot."

"Don't be afraid," Vail said. "We should just go. And survive from there."

"Easy for you to say," I said.

"What's that supposed to mean?"

I didn't reply. Vail gave me a suspicious look before being distracted by a new text message. She grinned at the message, replied and rested on my lap, almost instantly falling asleep; I watched her breathing slightly. I squeezed her nostrils closed. She grunted and pushed my fingers away. I then covered her ears and she smiled and whispered, "Stop it," and fell asleep again.

When Vail finally woke up from whatever kind of dream she was having we stood up and walked inside the Gallery of Modern Art. We didn't say much to each other; in fact, we went our own ways, only bumping into each other once in a while to comment on a painting or sculpture we liked or didn't understand or found pointless or thought we could make ourselves. There were a lot of times when I would stare at a piece of art and think about nothing related to that piece of art: I'd think about things like my parents, or about Vail's teeth, or about this story I wanted to write or about this story that I wrote that no one had ever read.

We left the gallery and, holding hands again, returned to the river and walked along its footpath and headed towards South Bank's restaurants and manmade beach.

"Ever play any instruments?" I asked Vail.

"You've asked me that before already."

"I have?"

"Yes you have, Dean, you asked me when we first started going out. I swear, half the things I tell you don't register in that head of yours." She walked ahead of me, faced me and tapped my head. "What *does* go on in that head of yours? I want to know."

"Tumbleweed, baby."

She looked skeptical. "Tumbleweed?"

"And air. Air and tumbleweed."

"So you're saying you have an empty head."

"Yup," I said. "Nothing comes in, nothing comes out."

"That's great," she sighed, turning back around and holding my hand again. "I'm dating an airhead."

"There are a few benefits to dating an airhead," I said.

"Such as what? What could possibly be good about dating an airhead?"

"Well firstly, dumb shit people do a lot of dumb shit things –"

"You're not convincing me, Dean."

"And when dumb shit people do dumb shit things, more exciting things happen in their lives. Which means more exciting things will happen in *your* life."

"I don't need a stupid man," she said. "I've encountered more than enough stupid men in my life."

"There's no better type of man than a stupid man. If you think about it, all great things, like unconditional love, like being brave and starting a business – it all comes out of stupidity."

"I'm not young anymore. I need stability. I need a man who can take care of me."

"I can take care of you," I said.

"You promise?"

I raised my hand like I was in court. "I promise."

She looked downwards and pursed her lips – she didn't seem convinced, but I was too afraid to ask her why.

We walked quietly for a while. "So, assuming that you've already forgiven me for forgetting your answer to this question, what instruments *did* you used to play as a kid, Miss Vail?"

"As I said before, Mister Airhead, I used to play the piano."

"Oh shit, I remember now. And the flute, right?"

"Yes, the flute."

"I need to learn an instrument," I said.

"You should learn bass guitar."

"I don't know. Everyone who wants to be cool wants to play the bass guitar. And as soon as they get a bass guitar they tell everyone how they play bass, but in the end they don't even learn a single song and the bass guitar just ends up in the corner of the room. I need something more genuine."

"How much more genuine can you get than bass? Bass is hot."

It irritated me every time Vail said something was 'hot,' but I didn't tell her that. "I want to play an underdog instrument."

"An underdog instrument? How about a table? You can be a specialist in banging your hands on a table. That'll be nice and hipster."

"I'm not a hipster."

"By deliberately not wanting to play what others want to play, doesn't that also make you a bit of a try hard? When you try so hard not to be a conformist, you also become a conformist to the group who don't want to be conformists."

"Shit," I said. "You've opened my eyes. You have a point."

"You might as well just play bass."

"I might as well just play bass."

Vail giggled. We stopped in front of this small

Japanese restaurant called Ginga. She looked at the restaurant's large, vertical sign. "I never know how to pronounce that. Is it 'Jinja' or 'Ginga'? I've had friends who pronounce both."

"Does it matter? Everyone has the freedom to pronounce words however they want to."

"Yeah, but you still need a universal pronunciation of things for everyone else to understand what you're on about. You're a writer, Dean. You should know how to pronounce this."

"It's a Japanese word. I write in English."

"Even so," she smiled.

"I'm going to let you in on a secret: writers actually don't know that much."

"I forgot, you're an airhead."

We looked at the menu and it all seemed appetising to me. I told Vail that it seemed affordable and for some reason she rolled her eyes at that. We made our orders and sat down.

"Lucky it's not that hot today," I said.

"I don't know," she shrugged, checking her mobile phone and texting someone. "I like the sun."

"For some reason I don't."

"Maybe you're a vampire."

"A sparkling vampire."

Vail put her phone down and looked up at me and touched my hand, smiling a strange, dreamy smile. "I like sparkling vampires. I *love* sparkling vampires."

"You just ruined my day."

She shrugged. "I like *Twilight*, and there's nothing you can do about it."

"So," I asked her, "what do you want to do for the rest of today? I'm all out of ideas."

"For a creative person, you barely have any ideas," she teased.

"What's that supposed to mean?"

"You always just either want to drink or eat or complain about something. You rarely want to do anything outdoorsy."

"Hey that's not true. This getaway was my idea, remember?"

"After much pushing. I hinted about this for months."

"Whatever," I concluded.

We didn't say anything for a while. Our orders arrived: a bento box and chicken karaage and a bit of sushi. I looked at Vail, who was looking at her phone, and then I looked at a waitress who sort of looked pretty, and then I looked at some people who were walking past us. I quickly wondered what kind of lives those people lived and who really cared what kind of lives those people lived before paying close attention to nothing at all: everything in my mind became blank. Maybe I wasn't kidding around with Vail. Maybe I truly was an airhead.

We ate in silence.

"I'm sorry," Vail finally said after we'd both finished eating.

"About what?" I pretended not to know.

"I'm just worried."

"About what?" For some reason I found myself tapping on the table with a chopstick.

"About money, Dean."

"Money? Money's not important."

"Money's very important, Dean. I'm worried about your financial situation. If we stick together for the long run, how are you going to support me? I'm all good for both guys and girls being equal and all, but I want my man to be the guy who makes more, not the other way. I'm the one who's going to have the baby and I'm the one who's going to be pregnant and out of work for nine months. Who's going to support us? It's just the way I feel, and you've told me you felt similarly. I need someone with stability. I need someone with ambition. You know where I'm coming from, right, Dean?"

I was taken aback by Vail's sudden outburst of information. She was thinking about a baby? From my experience with girls I've learnt that whenever they ranted or complained to you about something, especially when they ranted or complained about *you*, you have to absorb it all in, patiently nod, and, no matter how emotional their bullshit rants or complaints make you become or how unfair they seem, you have to shred down and completely simplify everything that you want to say in return – say as little as possible, stay as calm as possible, no matter what. Speak slower. Swallow your pride and smile, because you can get revenge on her in bed. I smiled. "I told you, I'm going to become an extremely wealthy writer one day."

"That's not funny."

"I'm not joking."

"How long have you been writing for, Dean?"

"Since I was six."

"How much money have you made from your writing?"

"Well I got a few marketing and copywriting jobs from it. The money wasn't bad."

"No," she said, "what I mean is, have you made any money from your actual *writing*, writing? Like your stories?"

I didn't say anything. For some reason I imagined Vail, tears in her eyes, driving away from my place with all of her things.

"And these jobs you talked about. How long did you last in them?"

"About a year or so or maybe less," I mumbled, then said a little stronger: "Hey, it's the money from these jobs that paid for this trip."

"That paid for half of this trip."

"You wanted to pay for the other half."

"That's because I felt sorry for –" Vail suddenly stopped herself. We were silent for a while longer, so she added: "Where will you get your money from now on? From your writing?"

I wanted to yell. I wanted to tell her that she has no right to judge me because most of her money came from her parents. I wanted to yell at her for thinking so lowly of my dreams. I wanted to tell her that I was aware of all the problems and that I was afraid of losing her, of losing everything. Most importantly, I wanted to yell at myself because Vail was right. In the end my story was this: I was unemployed and I'd been rejected by publishers numerous times and I was going nowhere. Nothing was changing and I couldn't even pay for my phone bills and there were so many other guys out there, good looking guys with lots of money and nice cars and impressionable jobs and positive attitudes towards life and they were all going after Vail, all sprinting towards her, all pushing each other out of the way just so that they could have a chance at having her sit on their laps.

"I understand why you're upset," I said.

Her eyes were welling up. "Do you? Do you really?"

"But the thing is, you're only upset because I haven't told you my plan."

She looked sceptical, yet slightly curious. "And what on earth is your plan?"

"It's a complicated plan. But it's a plan that'll work, and it's a plan that'll change our lives forever."

"You kidding me?" I spotted a small trace of what I hoped was a smile appear along her mouth.

"I'm not kidding you."

"What's the plan? Hurry up and tell me the plan. Did you get a new job offer? You got a job, didn't you?"

I coughed a little. "So, are you ready for the plan?"

"Just tell me, Dean. Stop fucking around."

"Alright, here it is." I carefully put my chopsticks on my plate. I let a moment of silence consume us both before: "I'm going to win the lotto."

Vail sighed, and then laughed. "You're a dick."

"I swear. I'll win a million bucks. Maybe even five hundred million bucks."

"Five hundred million bucks?"

"I'll buy some new undies and then you can have the rest."

She grinned and leant forward. "You'll give me the rest of the five hundred million? You sure about that? Because I won't be afraid to spend it all."

"You would, wouldn't you?"

We finished up and headed to a bar and I ordered a beer and a wine while Vail ordered an orange juice and after the drinks we walked along South Bank's manmade beach and nearby swimming pool, commenting about how we both heard that the smell of chlorine is so strong there because all the kids like to piss in it. The sun was setting by then, and a sweet, peaceful sort of darkness began to hover around South Bank's walkways and lawns and barbeque areas.

I placed my arm around Vail's shoulders. "We make a good team."

"You really think so?"

"I really think so."

Vail started to say something, then hesitated and changed her mind. When I didn't ask her what she was about to say, she decided to speak again: "I'm going to suggest something corny and romantic and you're going to complain about it."

"And what would this be?"

"Actually," she sort of giggled, "never mind. You'll hate it."

"I'll hate it?"

"Yeah, you'll hate it like you hate a lot of things."

"I don't hate anything. In fact, I love everything."

"Bullshit." She pushed me away. "The other day you went on a rant about how you hated cinemas. No one hates cinemas except for you."

"I didn't mean it."

"Oh you meant it, buddy."

"What I meant was, I hate the smell of piss in

cinemas. Then I went on about how I hate how people would even consider pissing in cinema, and how cinemas could house a movie so bad that people would consider pissing in a public place, even if they know that some poor staff member would have to clean it all up. You know Jude told me he chucked a shit in a cinema once?" I said. I looked at her: her arms were folded across her chest. "Anyway listen, there are a lot of things I love. I love writing."

"And what else?" She asked.

"I love you."

"And?"

"That not enough?"

"Nope."

We stopped by a walkway that overlooked the Brisbane River. Naturally, the scenery before us looked different than it did earlier in the day: it was darker and it glimmered against the lights of the city in the background. "Anyway," I said, quickly glancing at a couple who jogged past us. "What did you want to say?"

"It's nothing."

"What was it?"

Vail leant into me playfully. "You sure you want to hear it?"

"I'm not sure, but tell me anyway."

"It's just that I've never been there before, and this guy used to promise me he'd take me there but he never did."

"What the hell are you talking about?"

Vail breathed in, and, as if what she was about to say something incredibly taboo, exhaled and said: "The Ferris

Wheel." She quickly leant back afterwards, looking at me with a nervous smile.

"The fucking Ferris Wheel?"

"Yes, the fucking Ferris Wheel. Never mind."

"The fifteen-dollar-a-ride Ferris Wheel?"

"You know what, it's fine, never –"

"I can't believe it. I can't fucking believe… that you thought I'll say no."

Vail giggled. "No way. Dean Blake, are you serious? You want to ride an expensive sappy Ferris Wheel with me?"

"I am very serious," I lied.

Vail looked happy. She took my hand and hurried me towards the large Ferris Wheel. It was glowing white and impressively large: it looked sort of alien. "You know what? I've never ridden a Ferris Wheel before."

"I have, during a carnival up in Townsville. It was nowhere near as large as this one." It was a pointless moment; I was young and I was with my brother, and we looked down and waved at some people and that was it.

I paid and Vail took a photo of it with her phone before we both hopped inside one of the large carousels.

"Up we go," I said, sitting on the opposite seat from her.

We both peered outside. "I can't wait until we reach the top," she giggled excitedly. "I bet we can see one of my dad's apartments from here."

"At the Meriton?"

"Oh yeah, we can probably see that one too."

"It's interesting how we love to see things from up above."

Vail glanced at me before texting someone. "I guess it's because we spend so much of our time on the ground that when we finally get to see the world from a different point of view, we get incredibly jittery."

"Who was that?" I asked, looking at her phone.

"Just some friend."

Vail put her phone back into her purse and we both looked at the view. The carousel was about halfway up by then, and everything below me shrunk slightly as everything above me slowly grew. There were a lot of purposeful and pointless things that were happening in the buildings in the city across the river. How many people were happy, how many people were having sex? It was all so quiet – distance had muted all of their stories.

I looked at Vail. Sometimes her face would piss me off and sometimes she'd make me feel at complete peace. What made me care about her? What made me worry about her more than the silent people in the buildings across the river?

"I want you in my life, Dean," Vail said as we reached the top. "I know we've got problems," she continued, and I know there was a lot more she wanted to add to that, but she decided to end it with this: "but I want you in my life."

"I think we should just be friends."

She slapped my arm. "Very funny."

"I want you in my life too, Vail," I said.

"Are you afraid of things?"

"Of what?"

Vail shrugged.

I placed my hand on her knee and squeezed it slightly. "Sometimes I think I'm like, repeating the same thing again and again.”

After the ride we walked across the now dim footpaths towards the cinema, which I supposedly didn’t like. Vail nudged my arm on the way there. “What do you think about relationships?”

“About relationships in general?”

“Yeah.”

“They’re okay,” I shrugged. “They change people.”

“What do you mean?”

“Being in a relationship means that you’re no longer really the one person. I remember this guy, this thirty-three year old guy I worked with once, he walked up to me and said, ‘Dean, when you get married, when you have kids, you’re no longer yourself.’ ‘What do you mean?’ I asked him. ‘If you’re upset, if you’re down, you can’t just walk away. You have to be a bloody role model for your kids. You can’t just run away, you have a mortgage, you have a wife who says she loves you. You’re not yourself anymore, you’re your family.’”

Vail sort of laughed. “That sounds kind of morbid.”

“He sounded kind of morbid about it, but he believed it’s something important you have to do in life and that you just have to fucking do it. I guess he had a point. For instance, since we’ve been dating, it’s no longer Dean at the party, or Vail at the party, it’s Dean and Vail at the party. When someone asks me how I am, they ask how you are as well. We can’t be ourselves anymore.”

“That’s a strange way to look at it,” Vail said.

“But isn’t it true?”

“I guess.”

Vail seemed deep in thought.

"What's wrong?" I asked her.

"Nothing."

"You sure?"

"Yeah."

"You look like something's wrong," I said.

"Nothing's wrong."

She remained silent until we walked into the cinema and looked at what was showing. I pointed at a few movies but she kept shrugging and saying, "Whatever you want." In the end we decided on watching nothing.

"Look, was there something wrong with what I said?"

"If you think there was nothing wrong with what you said, then there was nothing wrong with what you said."

That pissed me off. I wondered what kind of man I'd be like if I was a dad. I wondered if Vail would be my wife and if I'd ever yell at her in front of our kids. I pictured myself as one of those dads in those American TV shows who just sits down in front of the TV, reading the paper and drinking a whiskey and not saying anything at all. I hoped not. I hoped I'd always be there for my kid or my kids or whatever. I don't know; I can't tell if it'd be better or worse for someone if their dad was there for them every day of their childhood. Maybe it'd be worse.

We walked around aimlessly for a while, saying nothing, until we ended up at a bar. We sat down. I ordered a whiskey dry and Vail ordered nothing. I watched Vail texting people as I took sips from my drink. Eventually, by my second drink, Vail's body relaxed and she looked around the bar before looking back at me.

"Sometimes I picture me as an old person, and you as an old person," she finally said, picking up a wet coaster and playing with it.

"And?"

"And nothing." She let go of the coaster and looked at me again. "Who was your first love?"

"I don't remember," I lied.

"Well that was a fast response."

"Because I seriously don't remember," I lied again. "I mean, like, how do you even define love? My definition is always changing, and for me to confidently say who my first real 'actual' love is would be fucking inaccurate. I'd be lying to myself and I'd be lying to you."

"I know we've both had our fair share of partners. But I certainly remember my first love. And yes," she quickly added before I had a chance to speak, "I've always had the one definition of love. To me, love is suffering for a reward. It's putting up with fights and imperfections and the constant fear of loss to enjoy those subtle moments, like asking my man to carry my bag if it gets really heavy, or knowing that I have someone to come home to and cry to, or seeing someone I care about achieve a goal, and like, just having a photo of him to look at and smile at after having a fight. Do you get what I mean? It's about, like, going through pain to enjoy all those stupid little things that deep down, we all actually long for."

"I don't know," I shrugged. "Whatever." The lighting in the bar made Vail look even more beautiful. Her cheeks were slightly rosy and she had a look of conviction on her face that I couldn't help but adore. But she also made me think about Eva, about this one evening when she placed her hand on my cheek and smiled at me, and another evening, when we snuck into a golf course and she gave me a birthday present. I missed Eva terribly, but I wondered if Vail also thought of someone else once in a while, of another man, possibly her first love, holding her face or even being inside of her. I remembered all the guys I saw Vail with when we were just friends. All of a sudden I didn't want to know about her first love and hoped with everything that she wouldn't mention him at all. "That philosophy of yours," I said, "it sounds like you've said it many times before."

"I sure have. It's because I firmly believe that that's what love is." She put her hand on my arm. "Don't you just hate your first break ups? Everything is just so horrible."

"Yeah, and you can barely sleep and for some reason, after you break up, you keep coming back together –"

"Until eventually, it wears out and you break up for good."

"I remember my first kiss," I said. "It was with this girl I ended up taking to the formal. She always had this little moustache and no matter how many times I told her to get rid of it, she refused."

Vail slapped my arm. "You're cruel. You don't just –"

"Our teeth hit each other's and we laughed. It took me a while before I got it right."

"Who says you've got it right?" she teased.

"You did."

"Bullshit."

"You told me that I was the greatest kisser in the universe."

"I did not." She realised something: "If you don't know what love is, how do you know you love me?"

"It's a feeling," was all I said, which, fortunately, made her smile and change the topic.

"I enjoyed our getaway. Did you enjoy our getaway?"

"It was alright."

"I like today," she said. "Today was my favourite out of all the days of our holiday. We got to walk around and I got to wear this new dress and we were able to like, speak to each other more. We should have days like this more often."

"Are you sure you don't want a drink?" I asked her after glancing at my empty glass.

"I'm sure."

"Well, do you want to get high?"

"I don't want to get high, Dean. For fucks sake. You're ruining this. Why do you always have to ruin this?"

After I had two more drinks we walked to Max Brenner, where Vail ordered a chocolate fondue for the both of us. We didn't say much as we ate it; Vail looked around the restaurant in satisfaction and mentioned that it was the first time she'd been here. "The line was just way too long the last time a girlfriend and I were here, so we didn't bother trying." Vail decided to pay this time, and as we walked out of Max Brenner I thanked her and held her hand and toyed with the big silver ring on her finger as we headed towards her BMW.

"We're going to make it, honey," I said out loud, and Vail squeezed my hand tighter. I was drunk.

We sat in her car and decided that we'd call it a night: she'd drive me home and she'd drive to her home; she hadn't seen her parents in what she said felt like weeks. We were quiet on the way home, and once in a while I'd glance at Vail and once in a while I'd notice Vail glance at me. Her iPod was plugged into the stereo and set to play an entire album by The Weeknd on repeat; the bass from her car shook the entire dashboard, causing her sunglasses and cigarettes, which she'd always place beneath the windscreen, to rattle. The night drive was filled with green lights and our silence; Vail usually sped, but she drove slowly that evening. We stopped in front of my place; Vail smiled at me and said nothing. I opened my door, walked to the back and pulled my bag out of the boot. When I looked up Vail was standing there, in all of her prettiness. I took two steps towards her, kissed her, touched her face, said goodbye. She drove away, music blaring. I realised that we didn't smoke for the whole day, not even once. I walked to my front door.

The Girl Who Had Every Man

The girl who had every man was about twenty years old (she was older than all of we were) and she wasn't that good looking but she was really touchy and wore nice clothes and put shitloads of eyeliner on all of the time, which I suppose made her better looking than she normally would've looked if she wasn't really touchy and didn't wear nice clothes and didn't have shitloads of eyeliner on all the time, if that makes any sense.

A lot of guys introduced me to her. James introduced me to her. Jude introduced me to her. This French guy in a Santa outfit introduced me to her. Everyone wanted to believe that they found her first, that they won at something, even if it was all completely untrue.

"Babe, I can't let you in here wearing that shitty pair of shoes," was the first thing she said to me as she took a very brief puff out of her cigarette before squeezing it into her sink. I remember her being surrounded by all sorts of guys that evening, and I remember them all looking suspiciously happy. Fuck she was chubby.

I looked at my shoes and then looked back at her. "But I like my shoes."

"No one else does, Howie," one of the guys, the guy who invited me to the party, snickered. The girl then laughed, and, as if by cue, the other guys surrounding her all laughed in unison.

I didn't stay long at that party, but I was told what happened near the end of it: most of the guys took turns having sex with her. Like other parties, it started with one guy kissing her in her room. When this would happen, the remaining guys would exit the room and sort of form a line outside. This made her famous: if anyone was ever heartbroken or if anyone ever felt desperate, she was the girl we could all depend on. She was the girl who didn't need constant courtship or dates to kiss us back. She was the girl who gave us so many experiences to talk and laugh about, guilt free. She was the one girl, who, after all her insults, didn't judge us and happily welcomed us into her arms… or vagina.

I didn't see her for about a month until I bumped into her lining up for a movie ticket one afternoon. I looked at her closely: her thick makeup, which tried to conceal her pimples, made her face look whiter than her body; she had a slight moustache.

"I don't normally watch movies alone," I said.

"Like shit you don't, you loser."

"I don't. And how about you? You're all alone."

She ignored me and glanced at something or someone in the distance while putting her hand on my arm. Still looking at that something or someone, she laughed a little, as if she was in on some private joke. I followed the direction of her stare and found nothing.

"What are you looking at?" she asked me.

"I'm trying to look at what the hell you're looking at."

She shrugged. "You're weird. Pretty girls like me

don't date weird guys like you, you know."

"What are you on about?"

"Just go away." She rolled her eyes.

"What movie are you watching?"

"*Twilight*," she smiled proudly, and when she did she actually looked sort of alright, in a way. "I'm supposed to watch it with a friend of mine who's late. Want to join us?"

Her friend never came and we kissed about halfway through the movie.

"I don't like the way you kiss, baby," she said. I could taste her lip gloss and popcorn. "You definitely need my help."

I hadn't kissed that many girls then, but I knew in an instant that she was one of those girls who kissed at a level above the rest of them: a kiss wasn't just about a kiss to her – it was about the extra touching and the nibbling and the darting and the fondling and the whispering in the ear. I, on the other hand, was absolutely shit. As we kissed I opened my eyes, and in the background I could see an old man smiling at me.

She never answered my calls but when she'd invite me over I'd be stupid and desperate enough to skip whatever I was doing and see her right away. I'm an idiot, I know, but she had a strange way of drawing men towards her. She insulted them frequently and her compliments, which came in the form of an "I like your shirt" or a smile and a touch to the face came so rarely that I found myself constantly working harder and harder to get her to give me another one. I hated her deeply, but she was the only girl who'd look at me twice.

It wasn't always about hooking up. Although she'd

frequently promise sex, she wouldn't always deliver. Sometimes she'd invite me out for a date and end up driving me to a café with a bunch of other guys and in the end she'd go home alone, no matter how many times we'd call her and ask her to join us. Once in a while she'd drive over and she'd be crying, and after about fifteen minutes of me watching her cry she'd smile against the evening shade in her car and we'd kiss and we'd go to my room and kiss some more. Sometimes she'd ask me for money and I'd give it to her.

I obviously wasn't the only one who loved her. She had plenty of guys in her life, a lot of pissed off and obsessed guys like me. But there was this one guy who she loved more than anyone else, and I'm guessing it was because he gave her the same treatment as she gave us – I heard that he frequently insulted her and stood her up and never answered her calls. He was the only older man she'd ever been with. He was thirty years old and wore glasses and had short hair and a goatee and a simple tattoo of the word "king" across his arm and for some reason everything in the world reminded her of him. "That so looks like my boyfriend's dog," she'd giggle. "My boyfriend took me there already and it was shit," she'd complain. "My boyfriend never kisses me down there," she'd moan.

I threw a bottle at her once. "I hate it when you talk about him so much!"

She smiled, and killing her cigarette before moving her lips right next to my ear, she whispered, "I can't help it. He's hot."

The second last time I saw her was during my

birthday. She was supposed to take me out to a Chinese vegetarian restaurant she'd wanted me to try, but as I waited for her in front of her home for about an hour or so she gave me a call, drunk, and told me to pick her up from a party up north.

"Shit, it's your birthday today?"

I yelled at her, hung up, yelled at my phone and then drove as quickly as I could to the party up north.

The party was, as expected, full of guys. All sorts of young guys like me. One of them looked fourteen. The only girls I could really find were three bored, ugly looking women who wouldn't stop texting on their mobile phones. Nobody paid attention to them.

I didn't have to scan the party much to know where she was: she was inside the room with the closed door, the door with four guys lining up in front of it.

"She has a black eye and shit," one of the guys in the line laughed, giving the other one five. "Ever gotten sucked off by a Cyclops before?"

"Hope her teeth are missing. I heard she fucking bites."

"What if she cries? I heard she was crying and shit when Vinnie had a go with her."

"I'm going next, man. She's sloppy enough as it is."

"Sad cunt, we'll have her at the same time."

"Fuck you, man. I'm not into that shit."

"What's wrong with a little sword fight, bro?"

Everyone laughed.

"A pussy's a pussy, no matter how sloppy it is."

They bragged and giggled about her but they looked nervous. I cut in front of them and opened the door and found her in there with a guy I knew from high school.

"Fuck off, Howie," he yelled. "Shut the fucking door!"

"Yeah, fuck off, Howie," she mocked, smiling up at me teasingly.

I walked over to her, picked her up and grabbed her panties and skirt and ran the hell out of the house. A lot of guys yelled and swore at me but for some reason no one physically tried to stop me. It was strange. Maybe they were used to this kind of thing.

I opened the passenger door, placed her in my car, threw her skirt and her panties on her lap, closed her door and then walked over to the driver's side of the car, opened the door and sat on the seat. I looked at her while slamming my door shut: she had a black eye and an ugly busted lip.

"What were you doing with that guy? Why were other guys lining up behind him?"

She rolled her eyes. She began to open the passenger door and get out but I pulled her back in.

"Why are you doing this to yourself? Did one of them hit you?" I asked. "You have a boyfriend."

She laughed, putting her clothes back on.

"I'm serious," I said. "You have a boyfriend and you're, and you're letting people do all this shit to you. And your breath smells like cock."

"You're being a hypocrite. You're being a silly little boy."

"I'm not a little boy."

"You are."

"I'm not."

She poked my temple, giggling and

humming: "You're a tiny little boy. You're a tiny little boy with a tiny little dick."

I raised my hand at her. "I'm only two years younger than you are and I'll always be smarter than you'll ever be, you fat slut!"

Her smile vanished in an instant. "What did you say?"

"I'm sorry –"

"So you think you're smarter than me, do you? Prove it. Prove that you're smarter than me."

"That's not what I meant." She was about to open the door again, so I quickly tried to think up of something to say, something to rightfully justify what I just told her. But all that came was this: "I really, like, didn't mean it that way."

"Whatever." She put her hand down to her lap. "Are we leaving or not?"

"Who hurt you? Was it your boyfriend?"

"I'm not telling you," she said.

"Just tell me!"

"Promise not to tell anyone?"

"Why would I?"

She shrugged. There was a long silence before she sighed and lowered her head, playing with her fingernails. "Yeah, it was my boyfriend. But promise you won't tell anybody."

"Why did he hit you?"

She remained quiet. I turned the engine on, glancing at her to make sure she didn't quickly jump out of my car. She didn't.

For a while, I didn't know what to do. We just drove.

As we drove I asked her a bunch of questions that only became stupider and more desperate. "How was your evening?" "Why were you wearing that tonight?" "Why aren't you talking to me?" "Why are you crying?" "Why are you so ungrateful for everything I've done?" "Look, do you even like me?"

She kept quiet. Her sniffles were small, vulnerable, like a tiny abandoned animal of some sort. "Men are cowards. They're afraid to admit that the only things that truly make them happy are constant sex, constant praise and constant reminders from a hot girl that he is the only man she wants. If any of these rules are broken, then you men feel incomplete. It's disgusting. You're all disgusting."

"Not all men are like that," I said. "I'm not like that."

"Fuck you."

"It's true."

She leant into my lap, unzipping my fly.

"What are you doing?"

She said nothing.

"Your lip is busted, and I haven't showered all day..."

We drove on, not saying much at all. Once she was done I'd look at her now and then, hoping that she'd give me some kind of attention, and when she didn't I pretended to find other things by the road, like old buildings and dark houses and drunken couples stumbling around the highway, much more interesting. We stopped in front of her home. She muttered bye and kissed me on the cheek before exiting my car, slamming the door shut and hurrying off.

As I told you earlier, she always talked about her boyfriend. She talked about the songs in his car, about the perfume he had on his desk, about his short but friendly mother. She also talked about where he worked: he worked in a CD store near the city that was filled with people who pretty much looked exactly like he did. They all had tattoos on at least one of their arms, they all had a fondness for black shirts and they all had thick-rimmed glasses. But I knew how to tell him apart from the rest of them because he had a permanent scowl on his face and the inner edges of his eyebrows always pointed upwards, permanently giving him one of those annoyingly smug looks. He was the most irritating person I'd ever seen in my entire life.

I followed him on his bus ride home from work one day. The brick I brought with me was one I found in the front yard of my apartment block. I used to always pass it and wonder why it was there: it was a dirty, rough and lonesome brick that just sat by itself and didn't seem to belong anywhere. It fit perfectly into my hand; its edges were sharp enough to really dig into someone's face. I also brought an empty bottle of beer with me. When I was twelve, there was this one guy who used to always talk to my friends and I about how he'd "bottle fellas at the station". Every few months or so, all of us would crowd around him in awe as he'd brag about how he just bottled a guy in the city over the weekend. He wasn't just all talk, too – he'd been expelled from his previous school for slashing someone across the face with the edge of a broken bottle and once, near the basketball court, we saw him smash a bottle on a table and chase a senior across the school, calling him a cunt before gashing him across his arm.

As soon as we both hopped off her boyfriend's bus and as soon as I saw it drive off I pulled both the brick and the bottle out of my backpack, putting one in each hand. Raising the brick, I hurried right behind him and slammed it into his back (I originally planned to slam it into his head but I didn't realise how tall he was). He stumbled forward, so I slammed it into his back as quickly and solidly as I could about three more times before he turned around and tried to tackle me, causing me to drop the brick onto my foot, which in turn grazed my right knee; there was a sharp pain and I screamed "Fuck!" but I didn't have time to worry too much about what was happening; he was trying to push me to the ground so I stepped back and grabbed one of his arms, only to cause us both to fall down together. As soon as I landed straight on my back there was a thump and I gasped for air – I couldn't move and for some stupid reason I thought I'd been paralysed.

Frightened about what was happening, her boyfriend began to slowly stand up; the bottle was still in my hand so I slammed it across his face. He grunted, and for a silent instant we just stared at each other in shock. All of a sudden, I noticed a whole lot of blood burst out of his forehead. He screamed and punched me a number of times but after a bit of effort, I managed to slam the bottle repeatedly into his head until it finally exploded, leaving tiny shards of glass everywhere. I stood up, screaming at the bits of glass jutting out of my hand. He was writhing on the ground, his hands on his face, blood trickling down his arms. I think there was a piece of glass in his eye but I don't remember. I kicked him in the ribs about five or six times and stopped myself from stomping on his head. I'd never felt so guilty and proud at the same time. I spotted his glasses about a metre away from us and stomped on them repeatedly before picking them up and throwing them into the street. I returned to him. "Don't you fucking touch her again." I spat on him and sprinted off to my bus stop.

I called her a number of times after that, but as expected, she never rang me back. It wasn't until about two weeks later that she texted me, asking if I wanted to watch a morning movie and have some lunch with her.

"Sure, where and when do you want to meet?"

We watched the movie in silence. Usually, she'd be muttering things or asking me questions or texting someone or trying to fondle me all throughout the movie. This time, she merely stared at the screen, her eyes wide open, her mouth completely shut. She put her hand on mine.

"What did you think of it?" I asked her as we exited the cinema.

She shrugged. "Why did you wear that shirt today? It doesn't suit you."

We walked to a café nearby and found some seats. As she bit one of her nails while skimming through the menu, I glanced around: the café was pretty much empty except for an old couple saying nothing to each other on one table and a guy on his laptop on another. The waitress, who looked like she was about fourteen, was giggling about something with the waiter behind the counter.

"You know what you want yet?"

She surrendered the menu down on the table, as if exhausted by it all. "I'm not hungry. Just get me a latte or something.”

“Sure.”

“Thanks.” She bit her nails a little bit more. “How have you been, anyway?”

“Concerned.”

She smiled. “About what?”

“That black eye of yours.”

“It’s gone now, isn’t it? I’m a pretty princess again.”

“I’m glad it is.” I waved at the waitress, who nodded and walked over. “Can I have two lattes please?”

“Sure. Anything else?”

“No.”

“Are you sure?”

“I’m sure.”

I looked back at her. “Are you okay now? Is everything alright?”

“Why shouldn’t it be?”

“Don’t tell me you’re still with your boyfriend,” I sighed.

“What boyfriend?”

I pointed at her eye. “The arsehole who did that thing to your eye.”

“Wait,” she said, laughing. “I told you I had a boyfriend?”

“Yeah,” I said. “That guy who works in the music store. You talk about him all the time.”

“Oh shit,” she laughed. “I completely forgot. Don’t tell anyone this, but I just call him my boyfriend to scare guys like you away and make you jealous.” She poked my forehead, grinning at me teasingly. “*You*, especially. You’re not the best looking guy out there but you’re so cute when you get jealous."

"Wait a minute. He's not your boyfriend?"

She scowled at me as if I was stupid. "I just told you that he's not. Can't you tell I was just playing around? Why the fuck would I cheat if I had a boyfriend?"

"That's exactly what I was fucking asking you," I hissed. Our lattes arrived and I smiled and thanked the waitress, who said nothing and walked away.

"I don't get you kids sometimes," she said, annoyed.

"Then who the hell gave you a black eye?"

"I got it while playing hockey. I told you that already."

"You didn't." She didn't notice my hand shaking as I took a sip from my latte. I closed my eyes for a few seconds, opened them, looked at the ceiling. I imagined a place, a better place than the place I was in. I looked back at her: she was texting someone. "You didn't tell me that you got a black eye during hockey."

"Our team got into this huge brawl," she said. "Everyone knows that. I even posted about it on Facebook, didn't you see? It got a hundred likes." She completed her text message, took a sip from her latte and then finally looked at me. "Do you want to come to my place after this? My housemate's out for the whole week." She rubbed her foot against my ankle and grinned at me. "Plus, I'll give you a reward for the movie and latte you so kindly shouted me to today."

"Fine," I said. "Whatever."

Eva, Part Six: Kids

Eva momentarily stopped looking at her friend's backyard outside and glanced down at me. "I can't believe I'm going to be spending the rest of my life with you." Although we'd been dating on-and-off for over a year, Eva and I both somehow agreed to the fact that we were eventually going to grow old and pretty much die together.

"When we get married," I said, "our rooms better be a lot cleaner." Eva's room was a mess. It was always a stupid mess.

"I wonder what our kids will think if we never change. If we decide not to grow up and get our act together."

I thought about it. "They'll think we're cool for a while until a few years later when they'll realise that we were actually really bad parents."

"Don't say that, Dean. We're going to love our kids with everything we've got. At least I will, anyway."

"What's that supposed to mean?" It was about five in the morning and Eva was lying down on one of those long recliner chairs, huddling herself warm underneath her friend's blanket. I was sitting on the floor next to her. We were both facing a large, glass sliding door that overlooked her friend's backyard. I wanted to sleep.

"I'm still mad at you," she muttered.

"Well don't be. There's no point."

She adjusted her blanket. "You know how I feel about drugs."

"It was just a one off thing. Your friend's boyfriend offered. I was just being friendly."

"It doesn't matter. Don't make excuses."

"Well you smoke all the time and you don't see me complaining."

"Are you kidding? You complain all the time about it." She kept looking out of the glass door. "And I don't smoke all the time and I told you I'm trying to stop. Anyway, why am I defending myself? It's nothing compared to what you did. And don't think I don't know that you've been doing it more and more often. You're always drunk or you're always high. I hate it when you screw yourself up like this. You know I care about you but you keep harming yourself like this. What's wrong with you?"

I didn't say anything. Sometimes she'd drift asleep and sometimes she'd wake up and ask, "Dean?" and I'd say, "Yeah?" and she'd fall asleep again. I mainly watched the backyard; the sun was slowly rising from behind the shed and the trees and all these little things I didn't care much about, really.

Charlie And The Open Open

Sometimes you deny what love is and sometimes you find it. Ribbon had a stupid name. She was a mother of two and she worked in a factory that made the same thing over and over again. She told us all that she couldn't be bothered looking for a second job or even a third job but we all knew it was simply because nobody wanted to hire her. She was sort of pretty in her own right but what took me a year to get used to was fuckin cunt. She loved to call everything a fuckin cunt. She'd call a chair a fuckin cunt. She'd call a piece of fruit a fuckin cunt. She'd call her kids fuckin cunts. She'd call me a fuckin cunt. She had three cars and none of them worked and I always like to tell everyone, especially my parents and my brother, that she's never cried in her life. She was supposed to have three kids but then the middle child, the boy, died when he was seven or eight or somewhere around that age. The first time I told Ribbon that I loved her was difficult. But the millions of times after that was easy. Anyway this story isn't about Ribbon.

I quickly turned around from my steering wheel. "You know what?" I asked Charlie or whatever his name was. "You know what?"

Charlie remained still.

"I have something really interesting to tell you that I know you'd like. Aren't you interested?"

I glanced at Charlie again. He was completely still.

"Fine then. Honest, I won't tell you anything if you stay quiet like that. I'm serious. I mean it. It's something you'll really like, too."

Charlie didn't reply. He kept looking outside his window, at the road and the traffic lights and whatever else was out there. It'd been four days.

After about three or four or five hours of driving past houses and buildings and shorelines and all that I got a little tired, a little bored. Charlie still wouldn't speak. I parked my car and stepped out and pulled him out of his seat. There was no resistance, no screaming. Nothing. He looked up at me with an expression like he actually didn't mind me pulling him out of my car. Holding his soft hand, I led him to a corner store and ordered two meat pies and chips for the both of us. After paying the ugly fat lady at the counter whatever it was she needed, I walked over to a table and pulled a seat out for Charlie. He sat down; I glanced around briefly before sitting right down in front of him.

I watched Charlie eat. His hair was black and flat and he was unhealthily pale. I watched him just sitting there and wondered what went through his stupid little mind and what he'd actually remember ten years from now. I thought about questionable things, frightening things, but then I changed my mind. The place was quiet and there was no TV and the fat counter lady didn't look at us twice. I leant towards Charlie. "Aren't you scared?"

The little bastard kept eating.

"You know I can kill you? I can cut you up and you'll never see Mummy again?"

Charlie stopped and looked at me for a second before continuing eating.

"You don't remember my face, you hear me? You don't fucking remember it." I pointed my fork at him, trying very hard not to raise my voice or ram it straight into his right fuckin eye. "You're pissing me off. You don't get to finish your chips. You're a quiet little shit. When I was a kid people had to punch me before I shut up but you look like you don't even bloody breathe. You're disgusting." But in the end I let him finish his chips before grabbing his arm and pulling him out of the corner shop and placing him back into my car.

We drove for another hour, past a lot of yellow and skinny cows and lonely sheds and sunny and dry weather. When I was Charlie's age I thought that everything around me was from another planet, maybe Mars, maybe something further away from it. I glanced at him. I parked my car and we both headed out to a field where I hoped I'd be able to clear my head a little, think more about what I was supposed to do now. I thought that things would turn out easier and I didn't know why I thought that things would turn out easier. The sun made everything strange; the grass sounded brittle as we walked straight and up and down and straight and up. I was sweating but Charlie wasn't. His lips looked almost purple. I'd never seen anyone look that pale in my life. If he wasn't walking you'd think he was dead.

He said nothing as he held my hand.

"I'll tell you a really funny joke," I said. I smiled,

nudging him. "Are you ready for a joke?" He didn't respond, so I told him the joke anyway. "Did you know some people say ants hear with their feet?" I looked at him to make sure he was listening. "Did you know that? Anyway, to test out that ants could hear with their feet was this smart scientist. What he did was, he looked around his fancy little laboratory for an ant, and when he found one he picked it up and put it on his fancy little laboratory table and tied it up. Ants have six legs, you see, and this scientist, he chopped off the first two legs of the ant and then let it go and said, 'WALK!' and funnily enough," I bounced left and right as I said this, "the ant *walked*! So it was true! The ant had legs and could hear him say, 'WALK!' But the scientist stroked his chin. He was smarter than everyone else – he went to university, you see, and not one of those, those fuckin easy ones anyone could get into, either – so he concluded that he needed further testing. So he tied the ant down again and chopped its next two legs off."

Charlie was still facing forward, blank.

"Then, then, uh, the scientist said, 'WALK!'" I let go of Charlie's hand and rushed in front of him and imitated an ant walking as if its first four legs had been chopped off. I loved telling this joke, especially to kids. "And believe it or not, the ant kept on walking. But still, the scientist wasn't convinced, so he went and picked the ant back up and placed it on the table and tied it up so tight it squirmed in pain a little. The whole place now smelt like ant blood. You know that strong smell of ant blood?"

Charlie didn't look at me.

"So anyway, the smart arsed scientist pulled out his

knife and cut off the poor ant's last two legs. He then untied the ant and screamed, 'WALK!' but you know what happened?" I stopped walking and looked directly at Charlie. Charlie also stopped, but his eyes weren't on mine.

"Nothing! The ant just squirmed and squirmed." Grinning, I squirmed around like how the ant would've. "The scientist was shocked. '*WALK!*' He'd keep yelling out again and again. 'Walk!' But the ant couldn't. All it could do was squirm in pain. The poor smart alec scientist was pissed off because the theory was true: ants can only hear with their legs!" At this I laughed the loudest I'd laughed in days, months. I was howling but it didn't matter. There were tears but they didn't matter. I could hear myself laugh, I could even see myself laugh and I knew fairly well that children laugh completely differently to how they laugh when they grow up, but who cares? It was the funniest joke in the world.

The field didn't seem to end and it only became hotter and sunnier, so we turned around and walked an hour or so back to the car again. I started the engine and continued to drive us both towards I don't know, west this time. "When I was a kid everyone said I was nothing but a problem to everyone and I hated the smart people and the rich people the most." I rolled my window up. "Rich people like you and your fuckin parents. Some cunts said I was born dumb and I every day I try to prove them wrong, but people everyday, they always call me out on it. Ribbon tells me to show them that I can be smarter than them and I want to prove to her that she's right. I know I talk to you about her all the time, but..." I reached my arm back towards him and put my hand on his knee. I thought about her face and smiled. "You'll love her, Charlie."

The sun was almost done for the day by the time we parked at a petrol station. I pulled my handbrake up. Everything inside me suddenly levelled out, as if some ball shoved in my heart some time ago vanished and left me relaxed, plain, annoyingly tired. "You probably reckon I'm scared but I'm not scared." I stared at him through the rear-view mirror and he stared back at me. His skin was milky and his eyes were thick and brown and nothing. "You know I can take you to the bushes over there and rape you, you know what rape is right? You know I can chop your little dick off and make you eat it and kill you right? I can find your pretty little parents and rape them and kill them too, you know this right?" I slammed my fists into my steering wheel and kicked around and yelled all sorts of disgusting things and all the while I knew I was capable of anything, that everyone'd listen to me because if they didn't I'd happily hurt someone and the pain'd be horrific and it'd keep coming and coming and coming and I'd make sure that everyone'd suffer as much as I have. I cried for a while and I could feel Charlie watching me. He put his hand on my shoulder and then let go. I faced the little shit, hoping that he'd have an answer. "What've I done?"

After putting some petrol in my car I pulled Charlie out of his seat and walked with him to the shitty little building where you're supposed to pay. I paid the woman at the counter fifty dollars for everything and then begged her to use the phone behind the counter and after a while of begging and arguing and threatening she let me use it. I called Ribbon and hung up when she answered after three rings. I glanced at the security camera looking at all of us from the corner of the ceiling. The woman at the counter was crying.

Charlie and I quickly walked to my car and headed for town, which was by then a day or so away. I didn't bother trying to get Charlie's attention for the remainder of the trip because I knew for sure he wouldn't give me any of it anyway. It was evening now and everything was windless and dry. It was the longest trip of my life so I tried to sing it off. It was the longest trip of my life so I tried to think about life the same way I'd normally think about life when I wasn't in trouble. It was the longest trip of my life and I was disappointed and angry and sick, awful.

I parked in front of the shopping mall where I stole Charlie. People behind me were beeping because I'd parked illegally but by that point none of that really mattered. I opened my door and stepped out of my car and then opened the rear door and unbuckled his seatbelt; I picked him up and placed him on the pavement. I held both of his shoulders. "I don't know what to say to you. You've fuckin let me down." I looked at every part of his pale face. I would've loved to believe that I'd made him up. I would've loved to believe that I just had a problem with my head and he wasn't real. His eyebrows moved. His oily eyes swelled. "You need to learn to talk more. I don't blame you for anything and no one should blame you for anything so don't you bloody cry. You can't meet her anymore, okay? It's your fault." I told him to fuck off and kicked him towards some shocked looking people and hurried into my car. The city was the same as it was the day before and the week before and the month before. Except it was more crowded, and it was dimmer. I gave the finger to the driver behind me and stepped inside my car and put my seatbelt on and drove all the way home, to Ribbon.

We Fall Asleep So Early

I'm twenty-two years old and I love alcohol. I'm not an alcoholic, but I love alcohol nonetheless.

I should've written this story from the point of view of an eighteen year old to make myself feel younger. All the books that I've dropped on the floor of my bedroom are about old people who are sad. Old people who are sad and drink alcohol and smoke cigarettes and hang out at the beach from time to time. The one I'm reading now has a fifty-something-year-old guy who sleeps with a bunch of women, and the women are all young, all my age. He says he's frightened of a lot of things. I don't find fifty year old men attractive. There are men out there who I find attractive but I'm not gay. I just compare them sometimes, just like how I compare girls.

I've been living on my own. I didn't choose to live on my own. My family all went to do their own things. My parents are overseas and my brother is in the city, drinking wine and coffee with his girlfriend. I guess I could've moved into an apartment and made a few roommates. I guess I'm just lazy. I guess I don't have money. This morning I walked around the backyard with my sunglasses on and that was it. I had a bottle of wine, or was it whiskey, in my hand, and I sipped from it from time to time and that was it.

My room is kind of a mess. I cleaned it up the other day, but now, it's kind of a mess. Vicki's still asleep. She's sleeping on the floor in the other room, which isn't my room. She woke up earlier and said, "Did I fall asleep?"

I said, "You've been asleep for the past twelve hours."

She didn't say anything because she fell asleep again.

Vicki loves alcohol more than I do. She's not an alcoholic. She's my age, and she just happens to like alcohol. She's pretty good looking. She has a toe ring that she never removes. It was meant to be a normal finger ring, but her fingers are too small for finger rings. She likes denim skirts. I like that she likes denim skirts.

It's hard writing a story about your life when no one's dead in your life, when no one breaks up or has a divorce or an abortion or a drug overdose. Well, there are a bunch of dead and dying people out there, but they're not my close friends. Maybe I should befriend an illegal immigrant or a soldier or a feminist. I guess I could focus on all the alcohol I drink, but I'm not an alcoholic. I'm twenty-two years old.

I like to order scotch and dry. Not because I particularly like the taste, but because it's probably one of the only bar drinks I know the name of. I first learnt about it when I was with a friend on my eighteenth birthday. He said, "Order scotch and dry! It'll get you off!" It didn't get me off but I kept drinking it anyway.

I like to drink while I read books. It makes the words as interesting as the story. They hop out at me, and I falter a little bit. But then I get used to how it works. There's a certain way to read books without looking too nerdy.

There's a certain way to read books without being obnoxious. I wear sunglasses inside my house sometimes because I know it makes me look like a try hard, and people, passers by, they ask me, "Why?"

I think I used to like sport. I'm pretty sure I had all sorts of sports uniforms. I'd run around with a ball or a bat or whatever and I'd play sport. My brother loves sport. He's probably running around, a cigarette limping from his mouth, kicking a ball right now, playing sport. I think I used to like basketball more than soccer, or the other way around. People really cheer for sport. You've got to play sport the right way. Sport can be annoying sometimes.

I walked around the Valley last night, in this street that's a street before the river. Everything was quiet. I picked up a cigarette from I don't know where and put it in my pocket. I sat on the hood of a car and had a drink with John. It was Wednesday and it was midnight and we were the only ones awake. We stumbled around. John always laughs at my jokes when he stumbles around.

I stopped in front of my ex girlfriend's house and looked at it. Her mailbox still looked the same. Mailboxes generally don't change. Sometimes I tell girls that I like them. Neither of us are sure if I mean it. Sometimes I write poems about girls but they all end up being about sex. I wrote this poem the other day and it ended up rhyming, even when I didn't mean for it to rhyme. I tried to reword a few words, but the lines still ended up rhyming. I showed the poem to Vicki. She asked me why it rhymed. She told me that poems aren't supposed to rhyme. I told her that I couldn't help it and she didn't believe me. And then she asked me why it ended up being about sex. Vicki told me that she wanted to write a children's book. But then she changed her mind.

I should write that I listen to a lot of music, but I won't. It's always expected. You've got to like music and movies and travelling and French to be a decent young adult. Only aliens and racists don't like music and movies and travelling and French. Imagine how people would treat me if I told them that I didn't want to backpack around Europe.

The third girl I met last night, I think she had red hair. But it could've been the lights in the club that made her look like she had red hair. But she might have had red hair. She was younger than me, but she looked pretty. At least that's what I'll tell John. She looked me up and down and said that she'd never date a smoker. She could tell that I was a smoker even if I didn't have a cigarette. I could tell that she was smart. Her bottom lip looked a little round, if that makes sense, and it was always wet and it tasted like candy and shit.

Once, when I was with Vicki in a restaurant that I no longer remember the name of, I noticed a couple next to us. They ordered the same dishes as we did. They looked exactly like we did, except forty years older. The woman had a toe ring. I looked at the old couple. I looked at Vicki. I panicked but I kept eating.

There was this one morning when I woke up and I didn't feel hung over. There was a different, frightening feeling in me, so I closed my eyes and clenched my fists and tried to shut it all away. When I opened my eyes again, I wasn't sure if it was the same day. Everything around me looked the same but I wasn't sure if it was the same day. I don't think it mattered if it was the same day. I smelt my pillow, stared at the little threads.

"Why do you look like you're about to cry? Are you constipated?" Vicki asked me, giggling.

"Because."

"Because what?"

I shrugged. I really didn't know what to say. "I guess it's because, well, like, is this it? There are so many things going on in this world, and, like, is this all we are? Is this all we're supposed to do? Is there a book somewhere I should read? Should I watch the news more? I don't know anything. I don't know what to do. I don't know anything."

"We're happy," Vicki concluded. "I mean, we're alive, right? That's a good thing."

I guess I like a few things. I like alcohol. I like the way my sunglasses fold. I like calling people up. I like stepping out of the shower. I like the word August. I like parties. I like driving to the beach from time to time. I like telling people I'm applying for jobs. I like girls, how they look. I like sitting down outside and watching things clear up, the sun rise and filter through the neighbourhood. I like how when I ask people, "How are you?" They say, "Good, and yourself?" And they don't notice this, but for a millisecond before I respond, I think of everything in my life, and I think of what people expect out of it, and I think of what people expect out of me, and I look inside my pockets for something to say, a lie or maybe the truth or maybe something in between, and from somewhere inside their shallow depths comes something, something supposedly tremendous, a word, I think, a word that's kind of invisible, but whatever, I'm not sure, and it's this: "Good."

Eva, Part Seven: Music CDs

There were a lot of things going on in the world and there were a lot of things going on in my life. But in the end there were constants, like the sun rising or the moon rising or plants growing or whatever – yeah, I knew they wouldn't have been there forever, but I was sure we could've depended on them with confidence for a little while, a few years, at least.

My Wednesday started at around two in the morning, at my old home. My mother was out that night and Eva and I, although we'd broken up over a year ago, found ourselves together again and we didn't have much to do except drink vodka and be amused by all the CDs that we found hidden all over the house, CDs that no one really listened to anymore. There was one particular box of CDs that we concentrated on: it was this green and dirty and dusty plastic box, and we tipped it over to pour everything onto the floor.

She picked up a CD and squealed. "Oh my gosh, Sisqó!"

"No way."

"Yes way. Remember *Thong Song*?"

"Of course I remember *Thong Song*. But it doesn't mean you should play it."

She ignored me and played it. As she sang and danced to it I downed another shot of vodka and watched her dance when I knew she wasn't looking, and when she finally glanced over at me, smiling, I began rummaging through the CDs again. Eva always had a funny way of dancing. It was like she was some kind of excited robot.

"CDs," I said. "Remember when people still listened to them?"

"I still listen to them."

"No you don't."

"What do you mean by that? Even if I listen to my iPhone I still listen to CDs once in a while."

"Don't lie to me." I picked up a CD with marker writing all over it. I grinned and showed it to her. "Check this out."

She walked over and took it from me, reading what was written on it out loud: "*To my baby Dean. We've just met but I want to be with you forever...* Oh my gosh Dean, is this Kathy?"

"No, it's from an ex-girlfriend."

"How many girls' hearts do you have to break before you realise that love is never perfect?"

"Shut up. She's the one who broke up with me. And remember, you're also the one who broke up with me." I suddenly remembered a morning where Eva and I sat on her bed, leaning against a wall, topless, staring at a green poster I bought for her from some weekend market. It was clumsily sticky taped onto her wall.

Eva poured us both two more shots of vodka. It was cheap, terrible vodka. We downed them in an instant; I watched her scowl and poke her tongue out. "This is gross."

I shut Sisqó up and placed the mix CD in. I turned to track six.

Eva eyed the stereo as it began to play the new song. "What's this crap?"

"It's *No Sound By the Wind*, by the Editors."

We sat still for a moment, listening to it.

I'll help you carry the load. I'll carry you in my arms. The kiss of the snow, the crescent moon above us. Our blood is cold and we're alone, but I'm alone with you.

"We've never really drank like this before," Eva said. "We kept saying we would, like we kept saying we'd do a lot of things."

"We've gotten drunk together before."

Eva looked at me suspiciously. "No we haven't, Dean. Even when we were together."

"Maybe you're right. Well tonight, we drink."

"Do you drink with Kathy?"

"Sometimes."

"I don't like this CD," Eva concluded.

"You've only heard one song."

"Let's change it."

"No," I said. "I like this song."

She scowled. "It's so boring. You're so boring."

"You're just being a dumb bitch."

"How about the CD I gave you?"

"You gave me a few mix CDs. You were very sweet. Remember the time when you were still very sweet?"

"I remember the CD you gave me when we first

started seeing each other." She smiled. "It was full of all these corny songs but I loved it."

I found one of the CDs she gave me – for some reason it had a Winnie The Pooh sticker on it – and put it into the stereo. The first song was *I Saw Her Standing There*, by the Beatles (it started with the line, "And I was just seventeen" – Eva said she chose that song because she was turning seventeen when we first met). I immediately skipped to the last track: *I'm Horny*, by Mousse T.

"We were such slutty kids back then," she said.

"We'll always be kids, full stop."

"I don't think we'll always be kids. I don't even think we're kids right now. We're more like surface children. We want to be kids so bad through the things we do and see and experience but we can't ignore the fact that the world is reminding us to become grownups every day."

I gazed at her intensely. "That's the most depressing thing I've ever heard you say. In fact, that's the most depressing thing I've ever heard anyone say."

"I doubt that."

We were both sick of vodka so I pulled out the next drink: red wine. I poured us both a glass.

"Since when did you start drinking wine, Dean?"

"Since you left me," I said.

"Very funny."

I didn't laugh.

After listening to a few more songs I replaced the CD with *Wonderwall*, by Oasis.

"This is the very first music CD I had," I told Eva as I looked over the album cover. "My brother and I both chipped in about fifteen bucks each to buy it. Out of all the tracks, I only really liked *Wonderwall*. Oh, and *Champagne Supernova*."

Eva stood up and sat right next to me on the carpet. I wanted to kiss her. "I've never heard of Oasis," she said, uninterested.

"What the hell is wrong with you? You've got to have heard Oasis before." I put the CD in and skipped to *Wonderwall*. "Listen to it."

"Oh," she giggled after a few seconds of it playing. "Yeah, I've heard that before." We listened for a little while longer before she added, "I'm getting a little dizzy."

"No you're not," I said.

"I am. But I think I can handle a bit more."

We kept drinking. I poured her another glass of red wine, which by then didn't taste as harsh as it initially did. Eva stopped *Wonderwall* and put in a Celine Dion CD in that must've been my mum's. We skipped a few tracks to the *Titanic* theme song, and, facing each other, we sang it as loudly as possible.

"You're a shit singer," Eva laughed.

"And so are you."

"Remember our theme song?"

I remembered our theme song perfectly. "We had a theme song?"

Eva slapped my arm. "Of course we had a theme song. I remember it because we made the whole tune up. We spent a few hours like, perfecting the lyrics and the tune."

"Really now." I pretended to try and remember it.

"You have the worst memory in the world." She looked saddened by this, but she leant her head on my shoulder anyway.

"Sing it for me," I said, leaning towards the stereo and lowering the volume.

"I don't want to."

"Sing it!"

"Fine," she said. She parted herself from my shoulder and knelt in front of me, putting both her hands on my shoulders.

What have I done?
Why are you here?
I don't deserve you, my dear.
I guess this is my punishment
It's the fear
Life's given me fear
The fear of you leaving me
Leaving me here

She sang it badly, but she sang it better than I ever could. When I met her she had straightened coloured hair and red streaks; that night I saw it for what it really was: wild, wavy, long. After some time her voice faded and everything was a stupid sort of silent; things were slow and focused and I was completely oblivious to every piece of bullshit in the world except for what my eyes could see in front of me: her eyes, her hair, her face, orange light.

"What have you been doing, Eva?"

"What do you mean?"

We kissed for a moment, and then stopped and had another drink.

"You're a bad person, Dean."

I didn't know what to say, so I said nothing.

I stood up and picked her up and spun her around. She giggled and mumbled something I couldn't understand. Not bothering to ask her to repeat herself, I let go of her and rummaged through some more CDs.

Eva suddenly leant forward and pulled out a CD she spotted. She smiled in excitement and showed it to me. "This is the last mix I made you." She skipped to the third track: *One Too Many Mornings*, by Bob Dylan.

We listened to it in silence for a while until she put her hand on mine. "Do you ever get the Think Effect?"

"The hell is the Think Effect?"

"I made the term for it up myself," she said, "but it's an effect that's very real. Have you ever been in those moments where you think about something so much that the world brings it straight to your feet?"

"I don't get it," I said. I truly didn't get it.

"Like once, when I really wanted this dress, I'd suddenly see all these girls with that dress on and I'd see all these ads on TV about this dress. Or when I'd keep thinking about you, I'd suddenly see a story of yours appear online, or someone would just ask me about you out of the blue, and then all of a sudden, you'd just magically appear in my life again. I really didn't think we'd see each other again, Dean, but I thought about you, I thought about you a lot, and here you are in my life again."

I didn't respond and she seemed okay with that. Instead I drank, and as I did and as Bob Dylan continued in the background I was overwhelmed with a few things: firstly it was guilt, then it was horniness, then it was gratefulness, then it was ungratefulness, then it was restlessness and then it was a terrible sadness.

I looked straight at my empty glass of wine when I told Eva this: "I blame you for everything, but I've always loved you and I will always love you."

"I love you too, Dean, but I'm drunk right now."

I pulled her chin up and we kissed again, and it felt terrible and great and it felt like nothing, all at the same time.

"You're going to remember all of this," she said. "And you won't know what to do with yourself or with Kathy or with anyone else."

"Which planet were you from?" I asked, stroking her hair behind her ear and kissing her more.

"Guess."

"Uranus."

"I'm from Mars," she said proudly.

"Typical."

"How's that typical?"

"It just is."

As I took her top off I wondered what would've happened if everyone's thoughts just spilt out of their minds and became reality – the world would be flooded with people having sex, with people winning the lotto, with murders, with anger, with secrets. If the entire contents of my mind were to have spilt out that evening, the only thing the universe would've seen was Eva. It would've seen her laughing at one of my jokes. It would've seen her crying. It would've seen her lying to me. It would've seen me holding her hand.

Eventually Eva had to vomit. She ran to the toilet and locked the door and I kept calling out, "Are you okay?"

and once in a while she'd reply with, "I'm fine." She eventually let me in and I wiped her mouth and put her on my bed. I watched her for a few minutes, hoping that she'd sober up and kiss me again. I kissed her forehead and walked to the kitchen and had some toast. As I ate I stared at the wall and knew that the morning was over.

Dirty Little Secret

Everyone is addicted to something. My addiction to something happened when I was eighteen years old and I decided to cancel coffee with Amber and go shopping instead.

He was about six foot something tall and had long hair and uncomfortably pale skin, and I instantly noticed him because he was standing there, alone, in *Sportsgirl* of all places. I secretly observed him as I browsed the skirt section, and after watching the way he just stood there, searching for nothing or nobody, I concluded that he wasn't there with a girlfriend or female friend or female relative or female whatever; he was just standing there, tall, alone, leaning forward a little bit, not saying anything.

"Hi," I casually said to him, pretending to look at some clothes nearby.

I expected him to reply with something charming, but all he did was look back at me with a shy little smile. He looked a lot younger up close; he had a slight baby face and seemed tremendously fragile. I guessed he was about sixteen. He was so tall he loomed over me – I could see a few nose hairs from where I was standing. He didn't look like he belonged anywhere in this world and this might sound a little funny to you, but I felt sorry for him.

"What are you doing here? Not shopping for summer dresses, I suppose?"

He said nothing, so I cleared my throat.

"Did you hear me? What are you like, doing here?"

He was awfully quiet, so in the end I purchased a skirt, took him by the hand and brought him to a nearby café, where I bought him a salmon pizza and chai latte. He didn't move much; in fact, he didn't move at all. All he did was keep smiling at me. In the end I had to literally cut slices of pizza up for him and feed them directly to his mouth.

"Salmon is good for you," I told him. "Keep eating if you want to be healthy."

After he hungrily chewed and swallowed each slice of pizza, I then had to lift up the mug of chai latte and pour sips into his mouth, carefully wiping anything that dribbled down his chin.

"Do you have anywhere to go?" I asked him after paying for the bill.

He sat there silently, looking up at me with a completely innocent, adorable smile. I remember that night clearly: I took him home with me and snuck him into my room and let him stand there in the corner, smiling at me as I slept peacefully, completely glad that a tall stranger was watching over me. He never told me his name, so I named him Jack, after all the action heroes in the movies I used to watch with my dad as a kid.

He couldn't hide in my room forever, so naturally I found him a place to live in. I used like eighty percent of my allowance and what I earnt at my part time job to rent him this small studio apartment at South Bank. In the mornings I'd wake up early and drive to the apartment and I'd bathe him, shave him and feed him breakfast. I'd make him a sandwich for lunch and in the evening I'd return and feed him dinner. He particularly liked playing around with my mobile phone so I gave him my old iPhone. It's funny, because I tried giving him other branded mobile phones before that but he'd only accept products from Apple. It was a worthwhile investment though, because he clearly loved it: he'd spend hours using the phone, obsessively scrolling up and down Facebook, Twitter and Instagram, smiling at what he was looking at excitedly.

He also loved a lot of other things, like watching hours of gossip television, reality TV and *Family Guy*. He greedily flicked through any kind of magazine I'd bring over. What he loved most of all, however, was money. He didn't like spending it, but he did love looking at coins and bills in awe and stroking them with his fingers. It was as if money gave him strength. He was so cute.

I liked taking care of Jack. In fact, I loved taking care of Jack. The two of us together in that cosy little studio apartment – it made me so happy. This sounds silly, but I felt like a loving housewife, caring for her man. It was like we were a more realistic version of Ken and Barbie.

I did this for about three years. Sure, I had a lot of arguments with my friends and family about where I spent most of my time and my boyfriend, William, ended up giving up and leaving me for someone else, but everything eventually panned out. I was happy with my situation and so they all had to be happy with my situation, too. Nobody was getting hurt by any of it and they had to deal with my decisions because I was certainly old enough to make them.

That's what I thought for those three years, anyway, because, well, I used to believe that I was a pretty lucky girl. I don't mean to brag, but that's just the way it was. I had great parents, I had good looking friends, I knew how to dress well and I know this sounds like I'm showing off but it was true: I often got what I wanted, whether it be with relationships, with grades, with getting accepted into courses in uni, with jobs – it was as if everything was handed to me in beautifully wrapped presents, probably because I deserved it all. I wasn't a criminal or a drug addict or some girl who had an abortion or anything evil like that, so I believed that I absolutely deserved all the luck and constant happiness I received in my life and that I had every right to keep at least one secret, especially if that secret wasn't hurting anyone.

But I was naïve. I should've known from the start that good things don't always happen to you, no matter how polite or pretty you are. It's like you're only ever given one jug of good luck in your life, and every day, no matter who you are or what you do, the luck in that jug either evaporates or gets poured out, and once that jug is empty, all that's left is you and the world and everyone else who's fighting to survive.

That jug of luck of mine ran out the evening I spotted Jack looking outside our window. It was strange, because he'd never done that before. He always seemed content with everything that was inside the apartment.

Although it slightly worried me, I made sure not to show it. I put my hand on his. "Did you want to go out, honey?" I know, right? I called him "honey" once in a while by then. He didn't seem to mind. Even if he didn't show it, I think he appreciated it when I called him names like "honey" and "love" and "darling". I mean, why wouldn't he? It showed that I cared about him. You're going to find me weird for saying this, but I actually cared about him more than anyone else in my life. "Alright, we'll go, but finish your salmon steak first. It took me a while to prepare it, and I love watching you eat my cooking."

After dinner, I washed up and then dressed him in a black jacket, black pants, red gloves and black boots. I tied his long, wild hair into a nice ponytail and shaved his beard, which grew every few days. With his boots on he looked like one of those serial killers you'd see in horror movies. It was hot.

I held his hand and we explored the city at two in the morning. I know this sounds strange, but it felt right. The city lights and the quiet of the early morning and the crisp weather created a sweet tinge of romance in the atmosphere. If someone saw us both holding hands in the distance, they would've felt like they were peeking into the lives of two lovers posing in one of those mysterious oil paintings you'd see in the museum.

I'd become awfully attached to Jack over the past three years, and although he never verbally confessed his affection for me, I knew for sure that I'd become tremendously important in his life. I mean, I bathed and fed him three times a day, seven times a week, and even if he had every chance on the planet, not once did he leave me and our apartment. Sure, only *I* had the keys to the apartment, but he could've stolen them from me if he wanted. It's true. He was an honest, genuine guy.

But as I mentioned before, not everything turned out so well for me. Everything went downhill as soon as we bumped into Amber.

Amber was with William (my ex boyfriend) and Carl (her boyfriend and William's best friend) and they were all red in the face and drunk.

"I haven't seen you in so long, you bitch!" Amber hugged me and kissed both my cheeks. "You look so pretty tonight. I love that bracelet." She then turned to Jack, looking him up and down before shaking his hand. "I'm Amber. Nice to meet you. And you are?"

"His name is Jack," I said.

Amber gave Jack another look over before turning back to me. "So he's the one you've been spending time with."

I didn't know what to say, so I said nothing.

Amber grinned cheekily, placed her hands on her hips and faced Jack again. "Oh my gosh, she's been so secretive about you." She eyed his hands. "Nice gloves, Jack. Where did you get them from?"

"He has eczema, so he decided to put gloves on tonight," I said.

Carl and William both took turns hugging me and shaking Jack's hand. Carl was a dick and I didn't like him. He'd always been one of those big, rough kind of guys who loved insulting people who were smaller than him. He was a loudmouth who had an easily recognisable high pitched laugh – it was like he was an ugly, human hyena, and I'm totally not exaggerating about the ugly part. Even though a lot of my girlfriends would disagree with me, Carl actually was, in all reality, a very ugly person. His hands were too big and out of proportion and his teeth were all crooked and his body was shaped like a dumb caveman's; he always had this irritating, jocky kind of slouch that only young girls who haven't yet experienced life yet could ever be attracted to.

William was completely different from Carl and I'd always wondered why they were even friends. Maybe because William made Carl feel stronger, more secure about himself. William, no matter how much sport he played or how many gym sessions he had, always remained scrawny. He wore indie shirts with strange slogans on them (like *Daft is__branDed*) and loved to read books that no one had ever heard of before. He loved watching those gory horror movies I couldn't stand and laughed at cartoons like *Adventure Time*, which I didn't get at all. He had a lot of freckles and big, puffy, curly hair. He was a listener, an introvert and someone who was completely into the flute as a teenager. He was really cute, too.

Carl put his arm around Amber, scanning my legs and cleavage over before finally looking at my face. "So you gonna join us tonight?"

"No," I said, quickly glancing at Jack, "we're just about to head home."

"No, you're joining us, babe," Amber said, pulling my arm, "we haven't seen you guys in ages."

"That's alright," I tried to say. "I'm a little sleepy, and Jack needs to get home. I'll text you?"

"You always say you'll text me but you never do," Amber whined. She was swaying and her hair was a little messy. Her skirt was as short as ever; whenever a group of guys would walk past us, they'd look her up and down. "Don't be silly. We have to catch up."

After a lot of debating we ended up in a maxi cab on the way to some house party that Carl wanted us all to go to.

I looked at Jack, who was staring at Amber, Carl and William with a smile on his face. "I'm so sorry," I whispered to him.

"How have you been?" William suddenly asked me.

"Good," I smiled. "How about you?"

"I've been good, too."

Carl grinned and put his arm around him. "He's been more than good. He's been really fucking good. You should see his latest girlfriend. She's hot, isn't she, bro?"

William smiled at me and, with hesitation, said, "Yeah, she's my girlfriend, so… Anyway, what have you been up to?"

"Yeah, what have you been up to?" Carl added loudly.

"I've just been busy with work and uni." Seeing William again sure did make me miss him, but only by a little bit. Don't worry, no one was as important to me as Jack was.

"That's good…" As William and I continued to smile stupidly and talk about our lives I made sure to try as hard as I could to pay attention to what Carl was doing with Jack at the same time: after becoming bored by my conversation with William, Carl leant over to Jack and tapped his knee – Jack flinched, making Carl laugh.

"Relax, buddy. We're just having a night out. You were just staring off into space and I thought I'd get to know you more."

Jack said nothing.

"No offence or anything, but how were you able to steal my best mate's girl away?"

Amber nudged Carl. "Shut up, babe, that's none of your business."

"I know I know, I was just asking. Isn't that right, Jack? I was just asking. We thought William did everything for her, that's all. I mean, like, you look like a good bloke and everything but this dude, this dude, he did everything for her. Like, fucking, *everything*. He sacrificed so fucking much. That's why, that's why he's my best mate. I'll do anything for that guy because he'll do anything for his friends and loved ones. Fucking hell you're tall. How much do you weigh?"

"Don't mind him, Jack," Amber apologised. "He's just drunk."

"Look who's talking, bitch!"

"But at least I can keep myself under control."

"Bullshit you can, babe, you were grabbing my arse all night tonight. You should've seen her, bro," he said to the cab driver up front. "She was a total slut. Do you like sluts, Mr. Cab Driver?" Carl squinted at the cab driver's ID on the windscreen. "Mr. Rajeshi, Mr. Rajishinjigosomething?"

The cab driver kept quiet. Amber laughed. She had a very similar, hyena-like laugh to Carl. "I did *not*. That was *William*."

"You both grabbed my arse, you fucking perverts." He swayed his attention back to poor Jack. "Are you a pervert, Jack?"

Jack didn't say anything.

Carl grinned and motioned his closed fist up and down. "Do you beat off? You understand the term, 'beat off'?"

"Don't listen to Carl, Jack," Amber said. She pulled her iPhone out and took a photo of Jack. The flash from her iPhone hit him like a punch, causing him to flinch backwards momentarily. His eyes then followed her iPhone with an intense curiosity as she placed it back into her purse. He kept staring.

Amber smiled. "There. I finally have a photo of my best friend's new man. Now, I'll know he's real for sure."

"What do you do, Jack?" Carl asked, flicking his fingers in front of Jack after realising he'd been staring intently at Amber's purse. "You stare a lot, don't you? Do you speak, buddy?" Amber tugged on his shirt to shut him up but he shoved her hand away. "Fuck off, Amber." He swayed to Jack again: "I asked you, what do you do?"

Jack said nothing so Carl slapped his knee. "I'm fucking asking you, what do you do, mate? It's rude to ignore people and just smile at them creepily like that. Did your mum ever teach you to answer when someone asks you a question?"

I'd been with Jack every single day for over three years and not once did I hear him speak; in fact, I'd never heard anything come out of his mouth. Not even a cough or a grunt, or even like a sneeze. That's why I wasn't entirely sure if I was hearing things correctly when he looked back up at Carl with a type of smile I'd never seen and said, "I eat people –"

"He's studying IT," I quickly said loudly, interrupting my conversation with William midsentence while hoping

Carl and Amber were too drunk to understand what Jack may or may not have said. "Sorry guys," I said. "Jack has this throat thing and he can't speak much today." I should've asked the cab driver to take us home there and then.

"Yeah, he looks exactly like an IT guy," Carl grunted loudly. He noticed some people walking along the footpath outside, rolled his window down and stuck his head out. "Don't be a disgrace you fucking Indians. Put your turbans back on!"

Amber slapped him. "Don't be so loud. You're such a racist douchebag sometimes."

William snickered. "Who says douchebag nowadays?"

"What do you mean? I say douchebag. Everyone says douchebag."

Carl pulled his head back inside and rolled his window back up, laughing loudly. "I'm not a douchebag, bitch!" He sat down and touched the cab driver's shoulder. "Sorry mate, Mr. Rajej or whatever the fuck your name is, I'm not a racist. Sometimes your people are just fucking annoying. If you hate the country, just leave, you know? Like, it's cool, you can stay here and everything, we've got lots of land and shit, but just stop complaining about how you're treated and start speaking English with a normal fucking accent."

The cab driver didn't say anything.

"Calm down, Carl," William said. "You've abused him enough."

"Great," Carl complained, ignoring William. "This guy doesn't speak English, either. You'd think they'd be smart enough to understand the world's most important language by now."

"You're horrible, baby," Amber giggled.

The so called house party turned out to be a party in a hotel room, a smallish hotel room with a whole bunch of people in it celebrating some girl's eighteenth birthday. Everyone was dressed in formal attire except for us.

"Are we even invited here?" I asked Carl.

"Stop worrying about everything," he snapped. "Of course we are."

My initial plan was to step inside, say hi to people I may have met once or twice before and then leave with Jack as soon as Carl and Amber were distracted. But the party turned out to be a lot more fun than I thought it would be: I bumped into a lot of old friends, there was hot music playing in the background and there were lots of free drinks; I hadn't danced to good music or had anything to drink for what felt like forever. I'd completely forgotten how fun drinking and dancing and catching up with good friends could actually be. When I met Jack it was as if he and I both engulfed ourselves in this magical little bubble, and everything else outside of that bubble didn't matter. I didn't realise that taking a step out of that bubble, at least once in a while, could actually be worthwhile.

As I drank and had a few laughs with an old classmate of mine I realised that I'd completely forgotten about Jack. I glanced around and spotted him – he was with William and Carl and a bunch of other well-dressed guys and really pretty girls taking shots. He watched them all intently before taking a shot for himself.

I don't know why, but I immediately wanted to walk up to Jack and tell him to stop drinking. Was that the first time he'd ever had alcohol? I knew he was a grown man and that he deserved to party once in a while just like I did; after all, it wasn't just me inside that bubble of ours and in no way was I the jealous type – he could've done whatever he wanted with whoever he wanted because I trusted him. But I don't know, I felt as if I was responsible for him, if that makes any sense.

I know I sound like a hypocrite for saying this, but for some reason I didn't mind it if *I* did the drinking or the smoking (not that I was a hardcore smoker or anything) or the dancing because the damage would've been done to me, and not him. It's not healthy to dance or smoke or drink with strangers, you know. In the end I just wanted to hold him in my arms and feed him and protect him from all the bad things in this world. It sounds ridiculous, but I'm not going to apologise because that's just how I felt.

A girl put her hand on Jack's shoulder and smiled at him and said something that I couldn't hear. She then put something (was it a pill?) into his mouth and they smiled at each other. I was about to approach Jack and tell him that maybe it's time we went home but Amber suddenly grabbed my arm and led me to the balcony.

"Come, let's smoke, babe."

"I don't really smoke anymore," I said, trying to glance back at Jack. "I kind of quit like, three years ago."

"Yes you do, babe. You smoke." Amber put a cigarette in my mouth and lit it and I inhaled, and I know this sounds really bad, but all of a sudden I remembered how good a little poison felt in my system. But I didn't have time to enjoy the cigarette – I had Jack to worry about.

"So?" she asked me, bringing me back to reality. "Why haven't you told me anything about Mr. Jack? When the fuck did he get into your picture? I really miss you, you know, and this kind of hurts." I'd like to say that Amber was being a little bit more forward because of the alcohol, but she'd always been that way. She was the artistic one out of the both of us, and ever since I knew her, she was always the one who wasn't afraid to be the first one to express how she felt. This was a trait of hers that I admired and hated at the same time.

"I know, I'm sorry I didn't tell you any of this. It's just…"

"That Jack is a little strange?"

"Yeah," I said, glancing at Jack, who surprisingly downed two shots in a row. He was grinning a very strange, unrecognisable grin and his eyes were wide open. "I don't think that anyone can understand him as much as I do. Not even my family knows. You have to promise to never tell them about him, okay? Please, promise me you won't tell them. They'd kill me."

"Of course I won't tell them. I'm your best friend and I'll do anything for you, babe. But it's like, you never call anymore and have been deliberately avoiding me." Amber looked like she was about to cry. "I'm always the one who texts you first and you've always got some lame excuse not to see me. Sometimes, like last Friday night, you didn't even reply to me! And why does it take me being out and randomly seeing you for us to finally meet again? We grew up together. We were best friends, we were sisters. We promised we'd never let anything get between our friendship. I'll even fucking *die* for you, babe. I'll die for you."

I think I saw Jack's lips move as he stared at this one guy who kept trying to yell something at one of the girls: I think he said, *I want to eat your eyes.* "I'm so sorry, honey. You were drunk and rambling when you texted and it was like, three in the morning. I didn't think you needed a reply."

"I know you're still there for me when there's an emergency or like, whenever I have like these major fights with Carl or whatever, but at the same time, it feels like you're like, not there, you know? Your mind is always somewhere else, and now I know it's on that guy, Jack." She looked over at him bitterly. "What's so good about him anyway? What was wrong with William? At least when you were with William we'd still hang out."

I shrugged, putting my hand on hers. "I can't explain it." I could've said more, but all I could think about was running back to Jack. "Honey, just know that you're always in my heart. Anyway, I have to –"

"I want us to be BFFs again. I miss taking photos with you and talking about boys with you and laughing about sex. Since you've been gone… Lately, Carl, I don't know, I'm like, having second doubts about him…"

I pretended to look concerned. "Oh no. But you guys have been with each other for like, forever."

"I know but sometimes I just want to be free. I don't know. You know, the other day, his mum, his mum, like, his mum asked me what I wanted to do for the future. I've told that bitch so many times about my dreams and goals but she's not happy because it's not the dreams and goals that she thinks are ideal. She's so old fashioned and she's so fat and jealous of me. She wants me to stay at home and take care of the kids or whatever and become dumb like her. She doesn't get that I'm serious about starting my own online fashion business. I don't get her sometimes. I don't know why I put up with her, especially when this business is going to make me a millionaire, you know? Doesn't she understand how lucrative online shopping is now and how affordable boob jobs are now?" Amber took a long drag out of her cigarette before throwing it out of the balcony. She scratched her thigh. "Can you imagine it, honey? Me being as good as Gucci? But that fat bitch is over there, she's trying to make me kill my dreams. She has such old school thinking. She's always just such a bitch. Are you listening to me? And oh my gosh, I didn't tell you this because you barely pick up your phone now, but Carl and I had this massive fight the other night. The worst fight we'd ever had. Babe, are you even listening to me?"

"What?"

"Are you even listening to me?"

"Of course I am." Jack was drinking straight out of a bottle of vodka now. No one was with him. He was muttering something I couldn't understand as the vodka dribbled down his mouth. "What did you guys fight about?"

"He was like, '*Oh, why don't you just give me space sometimes?*'" She said loudly while scrunching her face, imitating what he supposedly sounded like. "He said this while he was out. On the phone. While he was clubbing. I was like, just at home on Facebook. I only rang him to say goodnight and that I loved him, that I cared about him. Seriously, was there anything wrong in me saying goodnight and that I loved him? So what if I asked him who he was with and why he didn't tell me about it? Aren't those normal girlfriend things to ask?"

Jack was now eating from a bowl of chips like a complete psycho. He was scooping handfuls of them out of the bowl and forcing them down his face. I'd never seen him actively eat anything before – it was usually me who had to put food into his mouth. There were crumbs spilling everywhere; a group of kids were looking at him and laughing. One of them stood up and, after a bit of giggling and encouragement from his friends, put one of those green Mexican wrestler's masks on Jack's head. To make things worse, Jack just left it there as everyone pointed at him and laughed. Would it have been embarrassing for him if I rushed up there and took it off him? He looked like a strange creature with it on: his pony tail exploded through the back of the mask; the front of the mask covered his entire face with bright red and green patterns and exposed only his pale mouth and big blank eyes. "I suppose…"

Amber shook my arm. "Are you even listening?"

"Of course I am. It's just –"

"And like, he doesn't seem to support me when I'm in need. He says he'll always be there for me, but was he there that night?" Amber hiccuped, then cleared her throat. "Was he there that night? No, babe, he was there in the clubs, probably eyeing some slut with his friends and getting drunk and not even thinking about me. Stupid fuckin' sluts. Why does this world have so many stupid fuckin' sluts?"

I nodded and nodded and kept responding with one worded replies until I noticed William and Carl walk over to Jack. William spoke to him with a concerned look on his face, patting him on the back. Carl just snickered drunkenly and mumbled something incoherent into William's ear. Jack didn't say anything to either of them – he took another shot of something.

"That's enough, mate," I heard William say before trying to calmly remove the mask off Jack's head. Jack grunted and swatted his hand away.

"What's wrong with you, cunt?" Carl yelled, pushing Jack. Everyone turned to face them. "No one touches my mate, especially you, you fucking IT cunt."

"It's fine, Carl," William said softly, glancing at a group of kids who were now watching them. "It was harmless."

"Fuck that," Carl said, pointing directly at Jack. "Fuck off, you faggot. You fucking weirdo, fuck off and go home. No one wants you here, cunt."

At this point Amber, the idiot, finally realised what was happening and turned around to see what everyone else was looking at: drunken Carl confronting drunken, masked Jack.

William kept trying to pull Carl away from the scene but Carl insisted on aggravating Jack, who simply stood there, licking an empty bottle of vodka in his hand, staring at him. Carl broke free and punched Jack right across the jaw – Jack snapped backwards, dropping his bottle of vodka as the back of his head slammed into the table behind him, smashing a number of things. A number of guys immediately stood up and began holding Carl back as he kept charging at him.

I screamed and hurried towards Jack, who remained bent backwards over the table.

"Are you okay, honey?"

"I like," I heard him say as he slowly stood up, laughing. That was the first time I'd ever heard Jack laugh. It was a strange, snivelly laugh that made him sound like a greedy old man. I couldn't believe it was him. "Again…"

"What? Did you say something, honey?"

Then it all happened in an instant: Jack, as tall and heavy as he was, leapt across the room towards Carl and landed on his chest, pushing him to the ground and knocking all the other guys out of the way. As Jack lifted his right arm a horrifying silence wobbled across the entire room – I'm making a lot of assumptions here and this may not make sense, but I could *feel* everyone's mouths drop wide open at the rare and horrific sight in front of them. Everyone was completely frozen at the shock of it all. The silence quickly evaporated when Jack shoved his fist into Carl's mouth, breaking all of his teeth inwards and leaving his fingers in there as he hungrily began eating his neck. Carl never had the chance to even scream; all that came out of him was gurgling and the rapid twitching of his hands and feet.

Everyone shrieked and everything happened so painfully and so quickly. There was nonstop screaming, there was nonstop crying, there was nonstop panicking, there was nonstop running. I remember the song playing in the background as this all happened: some remixed version of a Miley Cyrus song. It was easily the most memorable evening of my life.

William and I and a number of other kids tried to pull Jack away from eating Carl's body while Amber and a number of other kids tried to run out of the hotel room. But Jack wouldn't budge; he was literally eating Carl as quickly as he could – it was messy, and it was inhumanly fast: I could already see Carl's neck bone. Jack then slammed Carl's head on the ground repeatedly as he gnawed on the remainder of his neck, breaking his head open to reveal bits of brain and skull before dipping his face into it and greedily eating it all.

I whimpered, and then I vomited. There was blood all over the walls. There was blood all over all of us. Jack suddenly stood up, causing those who were pulling on his back to fall backwards.

"J, Jack?" I asked him, my whole body trembling. "Honey?"

Jack looked around, looking for my voice, as if I was floating somewhere; at one point he even looked at my direction – but he didn't look at me, he looked past me. It's as if I was invisible. His whole head, his mask and his pale skin and his ponytail, it was all covered in blood and bits of Carl. His eyes were wide and clear and hungry. Once again, everyone was frozen, stunned, afraid. Jack leapt on top of another person and I shrieked. This time, he tore the poor guy's arm off then proceeded to eat his face.

I glanced to the right: William had a knife in his hand. "No, William!" I screamed, but he ignored me and thrust the knife right into Jack's neck. Jack didn't flinch, so William stabbed him again, and then again, and then again. Nothing happened and Jack was beginning to look strange: he was growing and his clothes were tearing apart. His once pale, smooth skin looked like it was covered in gigantic boils that continuously leaked blood and puss. A gigantic, twitching eyeball seemed to be emerging from his chest. By then only a handful of us were left behind: there was me and some girl who were too stunned to move, and there was William and a brave group of kids who were trying all sorts of ways to stop Jack from doing what he was doing. But nothing was working. One of the kids walked backwards and started recording the scene with his mobile phone.

We began running once Jack proceeded to eat the third person. We sprinted to the door to get the hell out of there but for some reason it wouldn't budge open. One of the girls, I think the celebrant, was sitting right next to the door, her phone pressed against her ear, fear and hopelessness all over her face, eyeliner dribbling down her eyes. "It won't open it won't open why won't it open?"

This is just a moment, I thought to myself in my panic. This is just a moment in life. Whether I live or die, it doesn't matter – it's a moment. This is the present, but in the future, it'll just be the past. If I survive, there'll be plenty more moments, both good and bad, both innocent and frightening. When I'm old I'll simply think about this incident as one of those many moments that happened; I may not laugh, but it'll be history, and I've never really cared much about history.

William pointed to the balcony, and I told him that he was crazy and fucking stupid but we followed him anyway. Someone screamed behind us and we heard multiple snaps, like bones breaking, followed by gurgles, followed by Jack's horrible snickering, followed by more screaming. The screams that went on that evening weren't just like any type of scream you'd hear at a concert or rollercoaster, either – they were horrible, terrified screams, screams I'd never heard, not even in the movies.

We looked out of the balcony. "We're thirty storeys high. I'm not jumping."

"We have no other option," William panted, looking around for something we can land on. "Shit, the pool's too far. There's nothing. There's nothing we can land on. Where are the cops? Why aren't they here? Why is no one helping us?"

"I Facebooked my parents. Facebook everyone you love. Facebook them all. Please just make sure to tag me in your posts. This is it," some kid cried.

"Someone help us!" William yelled out of the balcony. "Someone help us! Please!"

Another guy fell to the floor, sobbing, rocking back and forth. "We're going to die, we're going to die. I miss my dad so much."

William looked at the kid before running his fingers through his own hair. His face was covered with blood and sweat. He realised something and looked at me. "Who is he?"

"What?"

He angrily pointed at the creature that used to be Jack. "Why is that, that, that whatever-the-fuck killing everyone?"

One of the kids looked at me. "You know that guy?"

"Why did you bring him here?" William persisted.

"Why do you want us dead?"

"I didn't want to bring him here," I said. "You guys, you guys forced us to join you. He's a guy I fed. I fed him everything. I didn't think he'd… I didn't know what he'd do… I didn't think it'd kill us all in the end…"

William was about to ask me another question but was interrupted by someone gasping next to us. We looked down at the kid before following the direction of where he was pointing: Jack was walking slowly towards us, a giant grin formed on his now crooked mouth.

"I can't do this," the kid wept into his mobile phone before jumping off the balcony.

"Leave us alone!" William yelled, quickly glancing to where the kid jumped off before looking back up at Jack. He was trying to look brave, but he was shaking. It was an inappropriate time for me to think this, but I thought that the way he nervously stood there, trying to look macho in front of me, made him look pretty cute. He raised his fist. "You can't do this to us."

"Don't do this, Jack," I added weakly. "I fed you. I helped you. I introduced you to YouTube. I," I paused, "I love you." For some reason I felt the need to quickly glance at William after saying this. He didn't glance back at me, though, which was completely understandable. He looked directly at Jack, who by then was very close to us.

Nothing we said to Jack stopped him. He was probably about eight feet tall by then – he had to cock his head to his side in order not to hit the ceiling. His black jacket was torn and his black pants were torn and his black boots were torn and his body was all red and wet with blood and other gunk. His mask had stretched but still hid the upper part of his face – the part that was exposed no longer revealed his pale skin and human teeth: his skin was now lumpy, brown; his teeth were jagged and long. He was literally a monster.

The song in the background changed to one I was once very fond of before that evening: *Night Call*, by Kavinsky. It was the main song for a Ryan Gosling movie I watched with Jack at the apartment called *Drive*. I thought it was a pretty weird movie and I didn't really get it and I only really watched it because this girl from work, a total Ryan Gosling fan, begged me to watch it, but I remember Jack watching every second of it with intense concentration; it was if his life would end if he didn't memorise the entire movie. That was the first time I ever properly held his hand.

Jack reached the entrance of the balcony and stopped. We stared at him while he stared at no one. William gave me one last pained look before eventually throwing a punch at Jack. Jack didn't flinch. He grabbed William's head and repeatedly slammed it against the balcony's edge before hungrily eating the back of his neck.

"No," I cried, "Please!"

Another kid jumped out of the balcony.

I was frozen. All I could do was watch Jack greedily eat William. By the time Jack was done, William was merely a nice shirt, bones and a disgusting pile of blood and innards. Jack forgot to eat one of his eyeballs so it lay on the floor, staring straight at me.

"What have you done, Jack? What have you done?"

I watched in silence as Jack quickly ate someone else.

They say that when you're about to die you see

glimpses of your entire life, all the way from the very moment you were born. None of that is true. As I accepted the fact that Jack would eat me alive I only thought about two things: what I'd look like after he ate me, and if he still loved me. For some reason I wanted to believe that all of it was just some stupid nightmare. I mean, why wouldn't it be a nightmare? Why would something so horrible befall a cute young couple who have done nothing but love each other?

Jack finished eating his last victim and looked up, at me. We stared at each other and my heart sank at the disaster of my entire life. He stood up and knelt down next to me. He stroked my hair. I was crying. I wanted to be a hero, to find a way to save lives that evening, but all I could do was cry. I couldn't stop crying. I hadn't cried in three years; it felt as though any pain I'd held back throughout that time had stored up and released itself just for that moment.

"How could you do this to me?" I whimpered. "This is all Amber's fault. She should've just let us stay at home. Why did you speak to Carl and not me? I mean, do you even still love me?"

Jack kept stroking my hair. His fingers were warm, wet, sticky. I looked at him and I missed him. I took his hand in both of mine and kissed his palm. He was no longer a monster. He had his pale skin and long, normal fingers again.

"Let's go home," I whispered. "Let's go home. I'll figure something out. We'll find a way to not get you in trouble."

Jack remained silent. He carefully pulled away from

my grasp and removed his mask slowly, exposing the clean, upper part of his wonderful pale face. He was smiling – snuggled inside the lines of his teeth was blood. His chest was moving up and down but I couldn't hear any sort of breath come out of him; I couldn't smell anything. He stood up, stepped onto the balcony's edge, looked at me one last time and flew away for good.

***

There are a lot of things I told Jack in our apartment. Once, I even told him what kind of woman I wanted to become. I certainly didn't want to become a bitch, but I thought it'd still be important if I acted like a bitch, at least once in a while, to certain people during specific moments in time, because as Amber once said, "Sometimes you just have to be a bitch to succeed in this manmade world." I told him that I wanted to work in marketing or something, for a huge publicly listed company like Proctor and Gamble that sends its employees all over the globe with first class plane tickets. Or maybe I'd work as a Creative Exec for a luxury brand like Louis Vuitton, and I'd get to wear cute, expensive clothes and be driven around in expensive cars every day. I was so excited about having my own driver! I reassured Jack that I'd take him wherever I went, of course. Well, as long as he didn't mind coming along with me.

This Is Not Hell

It's too embarrassing to tell you why I'm sad, so I won't. We're leaning against the wall of some dimly lit hallway of some student's house and the party, which was supposed to be a fancy dress cocktail party, has long gone – Jude and Renée and I are just the remnants of whatever the hell happened; I'd wanted to leave hours ago but I said nothing – I'd kept it all to myself and had instead become more and more irritated by everything. The three of us are in expensive business attire: Renée is wearing a short black skirt and nice heels and Jude and I are in grey fitted suits and black leather shoes. But none of this information matters.

Renée looks at me, looks at her fingers, smiles and breaks out laughing.

I throw a piece of rubbish at her. "The hell you laughing about?"

"That joke."

"What joke?"

She waves me away. "Doesn't matter."

"I want to get rid of my tie," I say.

"Don't," Jude says.

"Why not? The party's over."

"It just looks better that way. I want to take photos

later."

"Fuck you." I start undoing my tie.

"Don't do it, Dean," Jude says, pointing at me with his index finger. "I'm warning you."

I undo my tie.

"You're a dick," Jude says. He looks angry at first, but then being angry seems to take too much energy. "Whatever. It's your life."

"Hey," Renée slurs to Jude. "Put another one in my mouth."

Jude laughs, but he obliges. He leans towards her, pulls a pill out of his coat pocket and puts it in her mouth.

"Give her two," I say.

"Give me two," she says, grinning while biting her bottom lip. "GIVE ME TWO COCKS!"

"Have you ever been in a threesome?" Jude puts the second pill into her mouth and leaves his finger in there for a bit longer – she sucks on it willingly. He winks at me before pulling his finger out to pour some beer into her mouth.

"No," she says eventually. "Are they fun?"

"They're not," Jude shrugs. "But you know what? Everyone needs to experience it at least once, just to say that they have."

I look around the hallway. "The hell are we doing here?"

"We're having fun, Dean."

"Is this fun?"

"What isn't fun?"

I kick Renée's foot. "What do you think fun is?"

"Fun is family."

"Shut up," Jude says. "Fun is this."

"What's this?"

"Fun is living in the moment. We're living in the moment. Stop taking everything so fucking seriously."

"Sorry then, Dad." I give Jude the finger and seriously consider hurting him.

We leave the party about two hours later and when it becomes clear that I'm in no state to drive a car, Jude tries. He fails, so Renée tries. We nearly get into a few accidents so in the end we leave the car somewhere and hail a cab along some street. Renée and I keep trying to ask Jude where he's taking us but he just giggles, so we shrug it off and play around in the back of the cab – I even manage to tear her panties off from under her skirt.

"No, Dean!"

"Why not?"

She doesn't say anything.

We arrive at some place, but Jude insists that we shouldn't pay the cab driver so they both get into a huge argument and Renée and I just watch, wondering what we should do. Eventually Renée tells Jude to shut up and throws money – her whole purse, in fact – at the cab driver. He takes it quickly and swears at us and Jude gives him the finger and calls him a cunt and we make our way across a street to this house, this small house, and the door's unlocked and we have burgers with this transvestite and her boyfriend and Jude gives the boyfriend money (forty dollars) and the transvestite, laughing loudly, her mouth wide and open while winking at me, begins to slow dance on the table. We all sort of laugh and sort of don't as she strips slowly, seductively, emotionally, whatever. I pick up a glass of juice and throw it directly at her penis and she screams and Jude asks me what the hell is wrong with me, and I push him away. The boyfriend laughs and punches my stomach and I wince and groan and fall to the ground and Renée, kind of clueless, laughs the loudest I've ever heard her laugh in the whole twelve hours that I've known her. "I hate all of you!" I yell to them and run – no, I sprint – out of there and manage to find a cab driver, the same damn cab driver from earlier, and tell him to get me to a church.

"Are you sure?" He asks me.

"I'm sure. I'll actually pay you this time."

"Really?"

"What's wrong with you?"

He drops me off at this Anglican church and I pay him and when I walk towards it I realise it's locked, so I kneel outside of it and lean my forehead against what was probably a marble wall and cry. What's a good future? Is it a future with a family? Is it a future with wealth, with millions, with fame? What is a good future? I look at my hands and the tears and the dribble falling all over them. I imagine myself setting myself on fire and turning into a cloud. Soon I'll be driving home to Kathy, beautiful Kathy, the girl who always talks about me, my baby, my one and only, the Queen of my stars and the Princess of my damn dreams, and I'll stroke her hair and kiss her forehead and whisper an apology and kiss her cheek, and she'll wake up momentarily and giggle and say my breath smells funny and she'll fall asleep again, and I'll take a shower and while I brush my teeth afterwards I'll think about her as I stare into the mirror, at my bloodshot eyes, at my dry skin, and

I'll decide not to sleep – I'll cook her breakfast instead: bacon, eggs, toast, peanut butter, butter, milk, juice, water, some sliced apples; during breakfast beautiful Kathy and I will talk about books and world events and joke about a few things and she'll say, "Dean, I'm proud of you," and I'll tell her that life is supposed to be meaningful, that from now on, my stories, my books, they'll be about good things, they'll be inspirational, they'll start movements, they'll revolutionise and they'll make couples fall in love again for real this time, they'll make people stop wasting their energy judging and complaining and instead use their energy to make the world a better place, and I'll suddenly run to Kathy and pick her up and she'll scream and, laughing, she'll tell me to put her down but she won't mean it, and she'll kiss my forehead and she'll tell me that she loves me and I'll tell her that I love her too, with all of my heart, with all of my mind, with all of my penis, and that I can't wait to see her again tomorrow, and the day after tomorrow, and the day after the day after tomorrow.

Jude calls me and tells me that he and Renée are going to get me. They arrive an hour later and literally have to pick me up from a pile of dirt and vomit and bush. They slap me until I wake up in some café in West End. "Breakfast's on me," Jude says. "I think you made me pregnant," Renée adds. We eat in silence, only once in a while talking about how good our meals are.

Generation End

It was the end of the world but nothing was different, really.

Charlie still sold his daughter, Amie was still addicted. The man in blue still fired his gun. That woman we met at that party still wanted to be a model.

The boy still swam that lap, the woman said I do, the missionaries continued their missions, the companies paid their employees. Smart people remained smart and dumb people remained dumb. Babies were born.

People still yawned, and people still scowled, and people still smiled, and people still laughed.

And the president of that group spoke to his guests at the dinner table.

And us?

We were just like all of the above.

It was the end of the world and we were texting our friends. It was the end of the world and we were turning on the lights in our rooms and listening to some music. It was the end of the world and we drove to school, to work, to hospital, to the party, to the gym. Some said we needed purpose, but we said more money please. Some cried heartbreak but we cried move on. Some said ungratefulness but we said this is your fault. Some said be patient, and we said no. Some said cry, and we said no!

We were the ones in the messy hall. We were the ones in the well-framed club. We were the masses between those who wanted to help the skinny kids in Africa and those who were already dead. We were the iPhones and the Googles and the reality TV shows and the skinny jeans and the desire to be wanted but the desire not to be wanted too much and the downloaded movies and the millions of music festivals and the friends on computer screens and the burning need to travel to Europe or Thailand. We were the inwardly insecure and the outwardly insecure. We were the result of bombs and battles and terrorists, of Martin Luther King and Martin Luther King Junior, of a nuclear power plant in trouble, of some Pharaoh in some drawing, of millions of people dead, of scholars, of activists, of bums and beats and women in bell bottom pants and of burning things and of psychopaths. We were the result of the oppressors and the oppressed. We were the drinks every Friday night and Wednesday night and sometimes Monday night and Tuesday night and Thursday night and Saturday night and Sunday night. We dreamt of being CEOs at twenty but we kept waking ourselves up. We were the sex and we were the loathing, the jobs that we'd be quitting, the attention that we kept losing and the causes we wanted to be seen discussing. We were the girls who had a crush on that DJ. We were handsome, or at least tried to be. We followed the waves and pretended we didn't. We were the cheaters. We were the prayers.

We were the romantics and the disgustingly pragmatic. We were the blaming and the complaining. We were the result of years of tears – we were the reward of sacrifice, we were the victims of privilege. We were the job applicants and the gangsters and the racists and the feminists and the hipsters and the fashionistas and the actors and the bisexuals and the young mothers and the bloggers and the tradies and the homies and the yuppies and the tragically heartbroken and the tragically tragic and the politically correct and the musicians in beaten cars and the helplines and the quitlines and the buskers on the street. We were the last chapter, the ending credits, the expensive encore, the happily ever after. We were the point, the end dream, the favourite money, the secret vices, the untitled democracy. We had a purpose, and we could only read it when we'd become blind. We were the victims of freedom. We were history on repeat. We were Generation End.

Eva, Part Eight: The End

I met Eva for probably the last time when she visited Brisbane again about three years later. She was wearing this tight, short purple dress she found at her aunt's place and these yellow pointy shoes and for some annoying reason she pulled it off.

Nothing and everything had changed for her: she was still studying in university but had spent a considerable amount of time in Sweden and America and Korea and India through a number of exchange programs. I, on the other hand, had stayed in Brisbane, remained unpublished and had been let go from a number of jobs.

"Let me drive your car," she said after we had lunch.

"Fuck off."

"Let me drive your car!"

She drove my car and wasn't that bad. We drove and drove and talked about life. She put her hand on mine during a red light and it felt warm, endearing.

"I always feel so comfortable when I'm around with you. I feel like I can actually be myself."

"It's because sadly, we were meant for each other."

"Imagine if the world ended right now," she said. "It'd be just me and you in this car."

"That'd be horrible."

She giggled. "What is a fulfilled life, anyway?"

"A life that's completely opposite to mine."

"Here we are, so concerned about all these stupid things when there are so many more important things we should be like, accomplishing."

"Like what?"

"You loved me, right?"

"Did you love me?"

I pulled my hand away from hers before placing it on her knee and gradually moving it up her leg. I slowly lifted her dress up to see and touch her panties. They were pink.

"My car is better than yours," she smiled.

"Well that's because your parents bought yours."

"I bet your mum helped with buying yours, too."

I didn't say anything.

"So how's Kathy?"

I looked outside the window, my fingers still rubbing her. "We're not with each other anymore. Still with whatever the hell that ugly bastard's name is?"

"Nope."

"That's good," I said.

"Hey," she said, "remember the time when adults used to tell us that we were the future of the world?"

We both laughed.

I pointed at the traffic light ahead of us. "Turn right here."

She turned my car right and we parked in front of the shopping centre near her friend's house. We sat there in silence for a little bit. "Rosie isn't picking me up until about twenty minutes from now. Want to go to the shop with me?"

We went inside the shopping centre and walked around. "What do you think of that?" she asked me. "How's your brother?" she asked me. "Have you been to Aria?" she asked me. "Do you think I should continue on and do a Masters?" she asked me. She kept talking. She kept talking and asking me questions and moving her hands and wouldn't shut up. All I wanted to do was kiss her.

We found a pet shop and she picked up a small stuffed toy of a penguin and smiled, showing it to me. "This is so cute."

"It's a toy," I said. "Toys are supposed to be cute."

"I had a nightmare the other night. It was about that time when, you know, I cut myself after we had that huge fight."

"Which one?"

"I don't remember, but it was huge. You yelled so much at me. And I yelled back."

"It's the past, Eva. We're older now. We're in our twenties and you've found your happy point."

"Is there even such a thing as a happy point?"

"Of course there is."

"I hope you've found your happy point, Dean."

I remembered something. "The stuffed toy I stole for you that you left behind here. The big white bear. I brought it for you. It's in my car."

"That's sweet. But Rosie's coming soon and I can't bring anything else to Sydney. It's way too big, Dean. You can keep it to remember me, or," she scrunched her face, "you can give it to some slut you meet in a party."

"Alright, I guess I'll give it to a slut I meet in a party."

She put the small penguin down but I picked it up and walked to the counter and bought it for her. She smiled, looked it over and hugged me.

"What do you want to do now?" I asked her as we walked around some more. The shopping centre was a small one – we covered the whole place in about four or five minutes.

Eva read something on her phone. "Rosie's here. I have to go now." She looked at me and smiled. "This is it, Dean."

"This is it, Eva."

"Bye."

"Bye."

We hugged for a while, and when we remained hugging I tried to kiss her – she pulled away. "We can't."

"Why the hell not?"

"Because."

"Because what?"

"Because we can't." She frowned. Her eyes were watering. "Don't you understand?"

"I don't," I said.

"I missed you so much," she said, wiping her eyes.

"I missed you too."

She tried to push me away but didn't flinch when I didn't let go. "Did you really miss me?"

"You wouldn't know the start of it."

"Don't go telling people we were together today, okay? They won't understand."

"You're shit," I said. "You're a dirty shit."

"Goodbye, Dean. Keep in touch?"

I stared at her, at the small lines on her forehead and

at her lips and at her perfectly painted eyeliner and her eyebrows and her teeth and her hair. I don't know why, but I was in pain. One day, she'll only be a memory. I let her go. "Yeah, sure." I watched her head out of the shopping centre, put her mobile phone to her ear and hurriedly walk towards Rosie's car.

A Letter From Dean

Dear reader,

I hope you enjoyed reading this book of short stories just as much as I enjoyed writing it. It took a lot of time and sacrifice to get it done, so I'm pretty happy to finally see it available for people to read.

As you probably know, I'm an indie author trying to make it in this Big World of Books. If you liked Surface Children, feel free to review it on Goodreads and share it with your friends.

Once again, thank you. If you'd like to hear more about whatever the hell I've been up to, feel free to stop by generationend.com

Dean

More Works By Dean Blake

Generation End

We were the point, the end dream, the favourite money, the secret vices, the untitled democracy. We had a purpose, and we could only read it when we'd become blind. We were the victims of freedom. We were history on repeat. We were Generation End.

Follow the life of self-destructive writer Dean Blake and his misguided friends as they tangle themselves in a world of sex, drugs, love and everything else that comes in between.

Read the blog (and download free stories) at generationend.com

Keep In Touch With Dean

You can keep in touch with Dean through the following platforms:

Goodreads (goodreads.com/deanblake)
Instagram (@deanblakeauthor)
Facebook (facebook.com/generationend)
Tumblr (generationend.tumblr.com)

Did You Enjoy Surface Children?

Don't forget to review it on Goodreads.

www.ingramcontent.com/pod-product-compliance
Lightning Source LLC
Chambersburg PA
CBHW061033120726
47910CB00006B/2228